Before & After

Nazarea Andrews

Before & After

Before & After

Summary:

1. Romance 2. New Adult 3. Second Chances

For information, address Nazarea Andrews
NazareaFYI@gmail.com

Edited by Brianna Shrum
Cover design by The Illustrated Author
Cover art copyright©: Nazarea Andrews
Ebook Formatting by A & A Literary

Before & After

For Jessica, who never bats an eye when I bring her a story

And smiles through the panic when I change everything.

Have some Nutella, love.

Before & After

Love is laughter.

Sugar and sunshine.

Brothers and family and life

Crazy. Beautiful. Chaotic.

And you. Always. Always.

You.

Before & After

Prologue: Now

It's raining buckets and I don't want to go out in that. I stare at it from under the awning of the club and feel Lindsay sway into me. For a second, we both wobble and another one of the girls bangs against my side and I shriek, sure we were going down.

Lindsay rights me, pulls me close. I lean my head on her shoulder and puff out a petulant, "Bitch."

Her grip tightens just a touch and she laughs.

I haven't been this drunk since senior year of college, when we did Christmas at her parent's beach house in Key West. I wouldn't be this drunk now except she begged.

Hung over and washed out won't do for the wedding, and even after that insane night on the beach with Jell-O shots and beer funnels and tequila body shots, I woke up without a hangover.

And that's what you do, when your best friend begs the night before her wedding. You do her shots while the rest of the bridal party screams at the strippers and you slip her watered down beer that smells like piss.

You take the holy-fuck-never-again drunk, because tomorrow, no one will be looking at me while she prances down the aisle in white.

Well.

One person will. And he'd think this shit was hilarious. I giggle against Linds' shoulder and she bumps me gently. "You good?" she murmurs as we wait for the cab.

I smirk up at her, the world spinning unsteadily. "I'm fucking wasted."

She laughs softly and kisses my forehead.

"Lindsay, get in," one of the other girls calls. Lindsay leans past me and peers at the cab. It won't hold all of us, and I can feel a new tension settle over my best friend.

Lindsay doesn't have a lot of close friends. Partly because we came here, to this city neither of us knows, because of the boys. So we both started over.

And because when we have each other, and the boys, well, we don't need much else. But she's more social than I am. And she works at a small ad agency, where she's gotten close to the other girls.

So when she needed bridesmaids, of course she asked them.

I smirk as Lindsay shakes her head. "Y'all go. Peyton and I will grab the next."

There's a moment of rain-splattered quiet and then the girl—I forget but I think she's one of the Jennifers—shrugs and slides into the little cab, slamming the door behind her.

"What a bitch," I mutter.

She laughs, that real noise that I know like breathing. Not the fake shit she's been shoveling at the other girls all night.

"Stop it," she orders and I blink up at her. "You're thinking too much. You're drunk, Pey. Let go and enjoy it."

I lean into her, and murmur, "Wanna help?"

She laughs again, shoving my shoulder, and I giggle. "You are such a slut when you drink," she mutters.

I nod agreeably, and a cab pulls up. It's dingy and the driver is frowning at his phone even as he pulls to a stop. He gives us a distracted look as we spill in and the world sways. Lindsay tugs me against her as I whimper and she pushes my hair back, studying me. "The Embassy Suites," she says and he nods, jerking into motion.

Linds mutters under her breath and reaches for her seatbelt. "Sit up, honey. Belt. The rain is awful."

"Freaking mother hen," I grumble and she shrugs, implacable. I huff and shift to sit up and my phone goes off, the ringtone that only Rike has. I squeal and Lindsay reaches for me as I scramble for my purse, abandoned on the dark, dirty floorboard. I close my hand over it and hear her scream, my name a twisted noise that is almost unrecognizable.

It's the last thing I can't remember.

Before & After

Chapter 1: Before

The bar is riding the line of slow and dead, which is depressing as fuck, because playing to an empty room is always a little bit of a letdown. Scotty doesn't bitch. He doesn't give a fuck who listens, as long he has a mic and his guitar with me to back him up.

Scotty could play to an empty room, and still be a happy motherfucker. He's done it often enough.

Lamar swings by the bar with a fresh round of longneck bottles, and I stand from where I'm adjusting the drums to take it from him.

"Slow night."

He shrugs. "It'll pick up. You play, and it always does."

True. But it's been months since we had this low a turnout to work with.

Barrie's is a dive and that's putting it nicely. It's a fucking hole in the wall in a college town, and has delusions about which college town it landed in. It wants to be a bigger deal than it is. But it's our hole in the wall, and Lamar keeps the free beer coming as long as we keep the music playing.

There's even a sticky dance floor, coated with spilled beer and other things I don't want to name, and some nights, we manage to draw enough of a crowd that they pack that little floor and scream along to our cover songs.

And there's another reason we keep coming back. The real reason I keep coming back.

I take a beer and glance at the little booth that sits empty, almost forlorn, in the corner. It isn't usually empty this late on a Thursday night. She's usually here by now, and the absence strings nerves along my skin, making my foot tap anxiously.

Scotty is watching me, and I shove down the unease as I swallow more of the beer and tap my drums, a quick beat that pulls a low response from the small audience.

He gives them a sexy half smirk and I see a girl at the bar texting. I hit the drums again and he glances back at me. I cock an eyebrow at the girl and he grins, not the smirk he reserves for the audiences, but the shit eating grin I've seen on my best friend's face so many times. The one that promises trouble and good times, and the distinct likelihood of getting laid.

A grin crooks one side of my lips, and I nod at him. Slam my sticks together twice before throwing myself into the beat of a popular summertime anthem.

Scotty follows my lead, crooning about summer and trucks, beer and good times, and the girls who are pouring in off the street scream our names.

Scotty lives for this shit. He always has. For the high of the girls and the crowd, the ones who for a few hours make him forget that we're two months behind on rent. That everything outside the circle of bright lights is a world of shit and heartache.

Because here, it's not. Here we're fucking untouchable as they sway to our music and the beat I'm keeping with my drum sticks.

He loves this. And I get it. Not because I care about the girls—I do, in an abstract sort of way. I love it because for a few minutes every night, between covering the bullshit on the radio, we roll out a song that no one has heard before. Sometimes, they love it. Sometimes, I come out from behind the drums, and croon to the room, a song that bares my fucking soul, and even with the lights so bright they're blinding, I can see her in her little booth, hair pulled up and messy, eyes half-lidded as she listens.

It's the closest I've come to talking to her. Because I know better.

A girl like her isn't meant for me. She's poise and pearls, peaches and cream skin and private smiles.

I'm covered in ink and scars and trying to forget my own fucked up past, and so far below a girl like her that it's stupid to even consider it.

I do though. Every fucking time I see that tiny smile when I sing.

She doesn't know I write for her. But I do. It's the only way I've allowed myself to talk to her. At night, when Scotty and I stumble home drunk and high off the performance, when one of the barflies doesn't end up in bed between us and—sometimes—on the nights when one does.

Scotty changes the rhythm and I shift, matching him as he slides into a ballad, crooning to the crowd. A group of sorority girls in uniform outfits of tiny shorts, hooker heels, and tops that flash smooth curves are on the dance floor, writhing and singing along, and I wonder which Scotty will tap to come home with us.

She isn't coming in. It'll be the first Thursday night in almost three months that she hasn't been here and it bugs me. I want her here.

I miss a beat, stumbling on the rift, and Scotty sends me a sharp glance, kicking in with a solo to cover me. I shake my head once, and he shifts his attention back to the crowd as we give in to the music.

It's the third song of the second set, when I've shoved her out of my mind almost completely, that the door swings open and she stalks in.

She's out of place in a blue sundress and white sweater, an oversized bag at her side, her long red hair swirling around her face in a halo of angry curls.

She's fucking gorgeous and the sudden release of tension is almost dizzying.

And right then, I decide. Fuck all the reasons it's a bad idea. I'm tired of giving a shit about that. She can shoot me down if she wants—but first I'm going to give myself a shot.

***

"Your girl was late," Scotty rasps as we land on two stools at the bar. It's late and the crowd of sorority girls has thinned to almost nothing, although a pair is nursing Cosmos and watching us speculatively.

Surprisingly, Scott's ignored them completely.

"Need anything, boys?" Manda asks as she sways past, giving Scotty a flirty smile. He grins at her, letting his gaze sweep over her.

My best friend is a fucking slut. But with Manda, it's all flirting and no action. She'd take him up on it—she's made that very clear. But Scott doesn't fuck where he works, and Barrie's has been too good for us to risk screwing it up for a quick fuck.

Which is good, because I'd have to kick his ass if he touched her. She might be a little too friendly and a little desperate, but she's a cute kid and I like her.

"Bourbon, Manda," he says, and she glances at me questioningly. I nod and she pours the drinks. Scotty glances at me. "What are you waiting on?"

I shrug and grit my teeth. Scotty twists and gives her a look over his shoulder. "Fine. Stay here and keep Manda company. I'm going to introduce myself to your siren."

I jerk him back by the collar of his shirt before he can take more than two steps and throw him back against the bar. "Back the fuck off, Scott," I growl.

He grins, a challenge and a taunt in that expression. "Then make your move, Rike."

I snatch the bourbon from Manda and take a deep breath before walking to her table.

And wait.

For a long. Fucking. Time.

It takes almost a full minute for her to look up, almost long enough for my courage to fail. I'm ready to retreat when she blinks and looks up at me, her blue eyes widening a little as they find mine. She looks startled and sleepy, and as gorgeous as she looked at a distance is nothing compared to how fucking flawless she is this close.

There are freckles sprinkled across her cheeks and dusted over her nose.

I swallow a groan as she licks her lips and gives me a tentative smile. "Hi."

"Hi," I say, and then go blank.

Because in none of my fantasies did I ever consider we'd actually ever get to this point. And the smirks and smooth lines won't work—not on her. They haven't worked for any guy that's approached her for the past three months.

"What do you call a group of unorganized cats?" I ask and her eyes cloud, confused. She gives me a pretty frown and I grin. "A cat-astrophe."

For a second, all either of us do is stare, and then she giggles. "That is literally the worst pickup line I've ever heard."

I grin, "So you want me to leave?"

Laughter dances in her eyes. "Have a seat, Jokes."

My heart shoves up into my throat at the casual nickname and invitation but I keep my cool smile in place as I slide into the booth across from her. She pecks at the computer a few more times, and then twists it aside and reaches for her drink—a whiskey neat.

She normally drinks vodka cranberry, and I've fantasized about kissing that taste from her lips. My dick twitches and she watches me over the rim of her glass, lazy interest in her dark eyes.

"Y'all sounded good tonight," she offers.

My lips tick up into a grin. "As opposed to most nights?"

A flush crawls up her cheeks. "No! You always sound good. I'm just—"

I laugh and lean back in the booth. Her adorable embarrassment is too easy to provoke. "I'm kidding, Red. Relax."

"So how did you get involved in this? The band?"

"Scotty needed backup and it was fun. Something to keep me out of trouble. Neither of us are very good at doing shit without the other," I say, skirting away from just how true that is and how fucking co-dependent we can be.

"That's cute," she says, grinning.

"Yeah?"

"Guys don't usually do the whole BFF bullshit—not like girls. It's kinda cute to see a couple of dudes who are good friends."

There's a little part of me that wants to point out that we aren't BFFs. That we were forced together out of necessity and kept together to survive. But I don't. That's a little heavy for now, and I don't particularly want her thinking about my best friend at the moment anyway.

"So what are you doing here?" I ask, leaning forward and tapping the open laptop. "Most girls like you find a library to study in."

Her eyes narrow a little, and I get the feeling I'm wandering into dangerous territory. "Girls like me?"

Her tone is tight and full of warning, but I ignore it, offering her a lazy grin. "Pretty. Smart. Too damn good to be in this shithole."

Her lips twitch and I lean forward, into her space a little, and whisper, "You've been here for months, Red. Distracting and out of place. So tell me. Why the hell do you keep coming back?"

Her eyes are wide and her breath is coming in short, sharp bursts and if I lean forward another few inches, I could taste the lips I've spent months fixating on.

"I like the music," she murmurs, and I swallow my groan, because fuck if that isn't the most perfect answer in the world.

"And the computer?"

A flush flares up her cheeks again and she ducks away. I lean back, giving her room as I take a pull on my beer. She's fiddling with the swizzle stick that came in her drink.

"I write sometimes. And the music is a greatinspiration."

I was wrong. She could say something more perfect. I grin at her and say, "You might just be perfect."

"Might?"

I hesitate and then shrug. "Need a little longer to figure that out, Red."

Her eyes are still amused but a wary as she watches me, a finger circling the rim of her glass, catching the drop of whiskey from her last sip. She lifts it and licks the Jack away, and I swallow hard, chasing my groan away with a cough. "Go out with me," I say, suddenly.

"I don't date," she says. She leans back and I want to drag her back to the edge of her seat, force her back into the easy warmth we were sharing even as she slams walls up between us.

"Why not?" I ask.

"Because I'm busy and because boys are idiots and because school—I don't need to be distracted."

"You aren't too busy to drop by and listen to me play every week for three months. And I'm not a fucking *boy*," I says the last bit tighter and fiercer.

Her breath catches a little in her throat as she licks her lips. "Maybe I'm here for Scotty."

For the first time in almost two decades, I want to punch my best friend. Because fuck if he's going to get this girl too, after all the time I've spent watching her. I've never cared who Scott takes to bed. Usually we take them together—women are no different than any other thing in our world that we share. But the thought of him touching her, or her on her knees in front of him, makes me irrationally angry.

"Rike," a sweet, low voice purrs behind me, and I blink free of my thoughts to twist and meet the gaze of the girl behind me. She's all smooth curves and long blonde hair and legs for fucking days.

She went home with us a few week ago, and I knew even as she was in bed with us that it was going to be a problem.

"Scotty is flying solo," I say, turning back to Red. I can feel the sorority girl at my back, the indignant fury from her. Red is watching her with curious eyes, gaze skirting between the two of us. I ignore the huffy girl behind me and say, "You aren't. If you were, you wouldn't be talking to me."

Her eyes flicker with reserved amusement, and I lean forward, and whisper, "Please. Save me from the sorority."

Her lips curve into a slow smile, something mischievous and mysterious in the twist of her lips, and I want to see that smile every day. I want to know why it's different, and what makes it different from the smile she would give me half asleep and naked in my bed.

I blink, shake the thought. Focus on now.

God, she's fucking with my head, *hard.*

"Go find a new toy, Lindsay. This one is mine tonight."

That's what her name was. Lindsay.

"You'll like them," Lindsay says, a smirk in her voice, and Red's eyes slip past me, settling on the girl and hardening.

Shit. That's jealousy, and a part of me wants to fucking crow with victory.

Instead, I reach out and claim her hand, letting my fingers trace over the curl of her palm, bringing her attention back to me as I absently caress her hand. She watches me curiously for a moment.

"Friday. Pick me up." She reclaims her hand and scribbles on a note card, sliding it across to me. Then she grabs her bag, shoving her laptop inside as she slides out of the booth and across the bar. She stops Lindsay, and murmurs something to the blonde girl.

Curious, assessing eyes flick to me, but Lindsay only nods and turns away from me. Red smiles, and ducks out of the bar.

I glance down at the note card. Her handwriting is messy and strong.

And her name is Peyton.

Chapter 2: After

Sometimes, the loneliness
Is a physical blanket,
A tangible thing that wraps around me,
Like a suffocating wave that won't recede.
And then your hand,
Rescues me.
(Rike's poems to Peyton)

Noise. Quiet, steady, noise. It breaks the stillness, shrill and sharp, then gone and it's just a waiting silence. My eyes open, slow and painful, and I look at a fuzzing white ceiling, and the bright silver of a pole near my head.

Why the hell is there a pole near my head?

I open my lips to talk, to ask, and a body, one I hadn't noticed before, shifts in the corner.

Someone—a nurse?—looks at me with brilliant blue eyes, and for a moment, I can't remember what I was going to ask, because there are only his eyes and the questions there, and a scruffy beard, a sharp, angled face, and long hair that hangs like he's been pushing his fingers through it.

"You're awake," he says, and I remember that I was asking a question.

But I can't remember what it was. I think, struggling to hold onto the elusive question, and my eyes widen, panic slamming into me. Beside me, the shrill and sharp noise of the monitor that woke me screams to life as my heartbeat slams in my chest.

I can't remember anything.

***

It takes a sedative to calm me down, and when I wake, it's slowly, with no idea of where I am. It's dark, and I remember the light streaming into the room earlier, lighting his bright blue eyes, and the wild panic when I realized everything was a blank slate.

I feel it again, now, but the panic is tamer, not as sharp and choking. I shift to sit up in the hospital bed, and glance around.

My gaze lands on the nurse, sleeping in a chair in the corner. His hand is wrapped around a phone, and I wonder, inanely, if he sleeps in all of his patient's rooms, or if I'm special.

Tattoos snake under the pushed up cuffs of a long, silver-blue thermal, and I have the absurd desire to push them up and see what designs will be revealed.

I don't even like guys with tattoos.

Why is he here? I clear my throat, and his eyes fly open. For a moment, his eyes are sleepy, soft, so intimate it makes the breath catch in my throat, and I swallow hard. Then he blinks, and the hungry emotions are tucked away, and there is only concern there, calm and professional as he pushes out of the chair and comes to the bed.

"How are you feeling?" he asks, glancing at the machine briefly. His eyes flick over it, and his lips tighten before he reaches for a button.

I stop his hand with my own, and see his eyes flare wide before he closes them, and with a deep breath pulls away from me.

Stung, and strangely embarrassed, I tuck my hand back under my blanket. "Where am I?" I ask my voice shaky with disuse.

How long have I been here; how long have I been unconscious?

"St. David's Medical Center." He pauses, watching me. It feels like he's waiting for something, but then he adds, "Austin, sweetheart."

Austin. Why the hell am I in *Austin?*

"Where would you rather be?" he asks, his voice carefully neutral.

I blink. I hadn't realized I'd spoken aloud until he responded, and I feel heat crawling up my neck. His eyes drop to it and warm, and I clear my throat, looking away. Searching for an answer to his question.

Where would I rather be?

It's a blank page, my past empty and stretching behind me. For how long? I bite hard on my lip. "How long have I been here?"

"I think you should let me call the doctor."

"Why can't I remember anything?" I whisper, and tears sting my eyes. I blink hard and sniffle. He's staring at me, his face tight and remote, and I want him gone, suddenly. I want just a minute, to break down in private. Away from this stranger with his tattoos and eyes that see too much.

"Can you call the doctor? And maybe give me a minute?"

He inhales sharply, and I feel a flare of guilt, inexplicably. Then he nods, and steps away from my bed. "Of course. Give me a few minutes to find him. If you need anything—"

"I'll call," I say, and he nods.

I don't know who he is. Why he's here. Why he looks so strangely hurt by my behavior.

"Do I know you?" I ask, hesitantly.

His whole body seems to tense, and I want to reach out and touch him, to soothe the tight lines of his shoulders.

A tattoo is licking up his neck, a bird in flames, just visible over the collar of his scrubs.

"I'll be back with the doctor," he says hoarsely.

And then he's gone, and any answers he might have are gone with him.

It stings a little. Like I should know him, or why he was here—and I don't.

Why the hell am I a hospital in Austin? Why aren't my parents here?

Every memory I reach for is blank. A space where something should be. It's like who I am has vanished.

The doctor is a Haitian man with skin the color of midnight and a wide smile. And an accent so thick I almost can't understand him as he explains.

The nurse—not Tattooed Blue Eyes—gives me a notebook, and when the doctor leaves again to find my MRI scans, I write what I know.

I was brought in from a car crash two weeks ago.

I had traumatic brain injury, causing memory loss.

Apparently, I was drunk before the accident and that didn't help my mental functions at all.

The girl with me is still in critical condition.

Her license says she is Lindsay Illian and I am Peyton Collins.

The driver died.

I live in Austin.

It's not nearly enough for me to work with—
to build a life on. But it's all I've got, so it's going to
have to do. What bothers me isn't that I can't
remember. It's that I'm alone here.

What the hell kind of life was I living, that I
am so fucking alone?

The door opens, and Tattooed Blue Eyes
enters with a paper bag. He eyes me for a minute, and
I stare back silently.

A tiny grin turns his lips, and he comes deeper
into the room and sits in a chair near my bed.

"Knock knock," he says, and waits, staring at
me.

I frown, "Who's there?"

"Hatch."

"Hatch who?" I ask, my tone sharp and
annoyed.

The grin blossoms into a full smile, "Cover
your mouth when you sneeze!"

I giggle and shake my head. "That's really bad, Blue Eyes."

His grin falters for just a second, and then he shrugs. "But you laughed. Now. Are you hungry?"

I don't respond, and he doesn't seem to care, going to work pulling out a plate of fried rice and chicken with vegetables and spreading it all out on the table. He moves easily, almost ignoring me, but I can feel the tiny glances he darts at me.

"What are you doing?" I ask, when the plate is in my hands and he's back in his chair. The sleeves of his thermal have been shoved up, and I see stairs crisscrossing up his arm, and a brightly colored fish on his other, twisting through weeds and flowers.

"I'm eating dinner with you," he says. Pauses. "Do you want me to go?"

That possibility looms in front of me. All night, alone in this room, and nothing. No memories or knowledge to keep me company.

The thought is terrifying and I shake my head. Because whoever he is, he's a distraction. Someone to keep my mind off the emptiness.

"No," I whisper. "Please stay."

Chapter 3: Before

Scotty is strumming on his guitar, but without any real point or purpose, and it's grating on my nerves. I scrub a hand over my head, and breathe a curse. He misses a note and I glare across the room at him.

"Cut that shit out, would you?"

"Why are you fucking nervous?" he demands. "It's just a chick. Hit it, and let it go. Get it out of your fucking system."

I snort. "Because that's worked so well for the past few months. Don't you think if I could forget her, I would have by now?"

Scott drops the guitar to the futon we picked up from a girl he fucked before she moved to L.A., and stands. "I think you've been fixating on her since the first time she walked into Barrie's. For fuck's sake, man, you turned down Lindsay."

He hadn't. And Lindsay is a little bit indiscriminate—she was just as happy coming back to the apartment to fuck Scott as she had been when we were both on the table.

It did make the next morning awkward.

"Can we keep her out of this?" I demand. Scott's eyebrows climb, but he doesn't argue as I reach into the almost empty fridge for a beer. My nerves are dancing.

"Text her, dude," Scott says, and his tone is somewhere between amusedly resigned and annoyed. I glance at him, and he extends the phone.

"She's outta my league," I mumble, and take a pull on the beer. It's shitty, lukewarm Bud Light but it's what we had the money for this week.

"Fuck you," Scotty spits, and stalks from the room. I swallow the beer and follow him. He's in the back bedroom, the one that's ostensibly his, but rarely used.

"You know what I mean," I grit out.

"And I'm fucking sick of it. We aren't that shit anymore, Rike. Get it through your fucking head."

"We aren't country club socialites either," I snap.

Scotty gives me a disgusted look. I get it. I've known Scott longer than anyone else in my life. With our history, I know exactly what he's thinking.

We've fought a long time to get away from the past we share. And for the most part, we have. Scott left it behind, threw himself into his work and his music. He'd forget it completely.

I can't. I've never been able to forget where we came from, or why we can't ever be more than that shit. It's why I've stayed away from Peyton.

"You let them win," Scott says, grabbing a shirt and pulling it over his head. It ruffles his blonde hair, giving him the just-fucked tousle girls can't keep their hands off. "Every fucking time you say we can't be more, you let them win. And I'm fucking tired of that. We're out—no one gets to decide what we are except us. If we want to be damn rock stars, that's on us. If you want Red, that's on you. But no one can take that shit from you but you."

He stares at me, green eyes brilliant and furious, and I swallow hard. Nod. I dig my phone out and tap out a quick message. A stupid knock-knock joke I heard a few days ago on the morning show.

Hold it up for Scotty to see. "Happy?"

He grunts, and pushes past me. "It's a start."

He's pissy and he'll sulk for a few days. I expect it. I knew he would when I said it. I'm just stupid enough that I said it anyway.

The phone vibrates in my hand and Scott twists to give me a knowing stare. "That was quick."

"Fuck off," I mutter, and thumb over to the message.

P: Took you long enough. Was beginning to think I'd need to find a new bar to keep things from being awkward.

I grin, and type a quick response.

R: *I'm the one who got shot down the other night. Shit like that will hurt a guy's ego. Make it up to me.*

P*: How?*

I hesitate for a moment, and then.

R: *Dress casual. I'll pick you up tomorrow.*

P*: Slow down, Jokes. Where you think you're going to pick me up?*

Well, fuck.

***

She agrees to meet me at Barrie's after her last class the next day, and I sit on the bouncer's stool—not that we've ever actually used the bouncer to turn people away. My leg bobs nervously, and I clench a hand on it to still the nervous energy.

Why the fuck doe this girl wind me up so much? It's more than just her beauty—although that helped.

It's that she's the first thing in a long time that I've allowed myself to want.

A car slows, a sleek gray Lexus and I see Lindsay, all straight hair and pursed lips as she watches. Peyton spills out of the car and shifts her bag on her shoulder. "I'll get a ride home."

Lindsay makes a small sniff. "Just call and I'll swing back by."

Peyton makes a face at her friend and steps away from the car, coming to stand in front of me with a small smile. "Hi, Jokes."

"Knock knock," I say.

A grin lights her face, and she says, "Who's there?"

"Lettuce."

She rolls her eyes and I nudge her with the toe of my boot. "Lettuce who?"

"Lettuce in please; it's cold outside."

"That's horrible," she says, but there's a sparkle of laughter in her eyes.

I push off the stool. She's wearing heels, but they still put her almost two inches shorter than me, and I'm struck by how tiny she is. With her big blue eyes and wild red hair, in a thin sundress and sandals with some kind of weird wedge that does fucking amazing things to her legs, she looks like a presence much bigger than she truly is. A part of me wants to scoop her up and tuck her somewhere safe, where she won't get bruised by the world.

Because I know a fuck ton about the way the world can bruise the innocent.

"Where you at, Jokes?" she asks, and I blink out of my thoughts to focus on her. She's watching me with curious, patient eyes.

No one has ever called me out like that. Pulled me from the dark spiral of my thoughts as easily as she just did—no one but Scotty.

I think I fall in love right then.

I shove that stupid thought down, and nod at the POS truck Scotty and I picked up a year or so back. I hold the door open for her, and she doesn't even seem to care that the truck is a rusted wreck. She just gives me a small, private smile as she slips into the cab. I shut the door behind her and jog around to slide behind the wheel.

"Where are we going?" she asks.

"A favorite place of mine," I say and her eyes brighten with curiosity. But she doesn't press for more as I put the truck in gear and pull away from the curb.

Keagan's is a record store, although lately he's been taking in boxes of old, used books. Records don't sell, not the way they used to.

We push into the store and he lifts his head to peer at me from behind a ragged copy of Playboy. I wave once and steer Peyton toward the back corner. A stack of poetry books sits next to the coffee pot, and I glance at it as I pour her a cup.

"This looks like tar, Jokes."

I nod and dump some shitty powdered cream in it before handing it to her. I make my own cup as I explain, "It's a rite of passage. Keegan doesn't really trust you unless you can choke down this shit. And it *is* shit. But I put up with it so I can come back here."

I take her by the hand and she doesn't protest as I lead her through the rows of crates.

Keegan doesn't organize anything. He just puts it out there and lets folks wander through it. "I don't know how long I've spent flipping through records and drinking this nasty coffee. A long damn time."

She steps up beside me and touches the glossy cover of a record by Aretha Franklin. "My grandmother loved her. We used to listen to her for hours while Grammy would make cookies and I'd frost them. Every time I hear "A Rose is Still a Rose," I can taste her cookies again."

I swallow hard, shoving down the pang of loneliness that rises at her words. Not her fault, and she can't possibly know why it stings.

I grab a crate and nod at the coffee. "Come with me."

Peyton give me an amused half-smile as she follows me to a small area with ratty couch. It looks vaguely like it was rescued from a dumpster after making a nice home for a rat family.

Smells that way too. For a heartbeat, as I drop onto the couch with a puff of stale old odor, I think I've fucked up bringing her here. Flawless and classy in her dress, she sinks down next to me, and kicks out of her wedges, curling up with her feet tucked beside her. "What are we looking for?"

I lick my lips and she follows the motion, and I know women enough to know exactly what that means,. She leans forward, just a little, and I get a peek of the gorgeous cleavage I've been trying to ignore. She smirks and taps the crate. "Focus, Jokes."

"I'm very focused," I say, my tone hoarse and hungry. Her eyes dart to me, and she hesitates for moment, but I pull back before either of us can act on the hunger that's running too hot between us.

Maybe I should have taken Lindsay to bed with Scotty. I probably wouldn't be so fucking desperate to get my hands on Peyton if I had.

"Nothing," I say, and force my tone to stay casual and even. "Anything. Nothing. We don't come looking for anything in particular, we just take what we find. That's the beauty of Keegan's; you never know what you'll come across, so you take what you find."

"When did you find this place?" she asks as I pull out a stack of records and begin flipping through them.

"When I turned sixteen. We grew up around here, and we both loved music. We had the freedom to roam then, so we'd meet here and flip through shit until it was time to go home. Keegan sold Scotty his first guitar—a broke ass piece of shit he picked up with a few dozen boxes of broken records. It was the only thing I've ever seen him give away, and I think it was mostly because Scotty offered to take the rest of the junk to the dump. We loved this place."

"You still do," she contributes, leaning over and snagging a bright purple record from me and examining it. She sips her coffee and shudders, before she sets it aside and studies the album artwork intently. I try to ignore her focusing on the stack in front of me. But it's hard, especially as she relaxes and more of her slight body weight leans into me, warming my side in the best possible way.

Her breath brushes against my neck as she leans across me and puts her selection in the keep pile.

"How did you get started on the drum?"

Keegan found a set of drums, a few weeks later. Looking back, we knew what he was doing. Keeping us together and off the streets. Out of the shit that was our reality. But at the time, it was just a weird coincidence that gave us another outlet. And as long as we weren't asking for money, no one really cared what we did.

It was one of the few bright spots of our life growing up.

"The drums showed up a little later and the rest was history. We played all the time. I didn't really care; it was for Scott"

She examines me for a moment, and then, "You are very close to him."

I nod, not bothering to argue or justify it.

Most chicks don't really get my friendship with Scott. Most either like us because we're into sharing, or they get annoyed because we have no boundaries. I'm pretty sure Peyton isn't into kinky shit, but I don't know that she's sitting in the second category either. And that's something I'm not sure I know what to do with.

"You're thinking again. Stay with me," she murmurs, squeezing my hand, and I flash her a smile before I drop a stack of records in her lap. She makes a little noise of surprise, and I grin.

"Help me."

Chapter 4: After

Quiet. The darkness

Presses against me, the

Distance yawns between us.

Quiet. And in the stillness,

space melts away. And

there you are.

(Rike's poem to Peyton)

The shrink the hospital sends me to is a fucking joke.

She wants to try meditation and hypnosis. Because either of those will help. I've spent three days here and I know nothing about who I am or why the hell I'm here.

There's a tap on my door and I stop punching the pillow to look up as the door swings open.

He's back. He's been gone for most of the past three days, and I've wondered. I shouldn't have, but I've found myself pulled back to him despite my best intentions.

"What did the pillow do?"

I smooth it and flush. "Nothing. It didn't do— where have you been?"

He arches an eyebrow and grins at me, and I look away. He doesn't answer immediately, stalking deeper into the room and dropping into the chair next to my bed. He sprawls there, ridiculously comfortable, and I almost want to dislike him for it. There's a confident air that wraps around him. He's covered in tattoos—I can see them more with the tshirt he's wearing—and he smiles as if the world is waiting for him to grace it with his presence. "Did you miss me, sweetheart?"

The term of endearment confirms what I've begun suspecting—he isn't a nurse.

"I don't know. I don't know you so I don't suppose I could miss you," I answer honestly. His smile falters, and I feel like I said the wrong thing.

Like he is waiting for something from me. "Do I?" I blurt, suddenly. His eyes dart up to mine and his grin fails completely.

"Do you what?" he asks hoarsely.

I almost ask. I think he want me to. But there is something terrifying and deep in his eyes, something I'm not ready to face. So I make a face, and shake my head. Twitch my blanket over my cast.

The accident that stole my memory also shattered my leg, my left arm, and four ribs. I'm told I'm lucky. That the amnesia might pass, that the leg will heal, and my bruises will fade. I'll walk, and I'll lead a normal life.

"The girl who came in with me. Do you know anything about her?"

"She's still touch and go," he says, and something about his voice jerks my gaze up to him.

There's grief there. Surprising.

"Why are you here?" I ask, abruptly.

For the first time, he looks nervous. He rubs his hands on his jeans, and then leans forward, digging into the bag he carried into the room.

"I brought you some stuff. Books. Music. A couple movies are loaded on the tablet. And you can google shit if you want. I know that it's not your memory, but I want to help you. I want to do what I can to help you figure out who you are and where you come from."

He's staring at me, his face open and earnest, hopeful.

"What's your name?" I whisper.

Why does he look so sad? "Rike. Riker Johnston."

I smile and extend my hand, the one that is still hooked up to IVs, my fingers splinted and half-healed. For a moment, I feel a flash of embarrassment. But his hand, covering mine, is warm and impossibly careful, and I want to bask in the feel of it.

"I'm Peyton Collins," I says softly. Almost shyly.

"Hi, Pey," he murmurs, and it soothes me. I don't want to think about why.

***

We watch a movie and it's interesting, but when it's over, that's all it was. Interesting. Not a clue to who I am. But Rike laughs and it's relaxing, just hanging out with him. There aren't questioning stares from doctors and nurses, barely veiled sympathy that makes my stomach hurt.

He's just present.

When the movie ends, the night is dark outside my window. He stretches and stands. "I should go. I'm surprised they haven't kicked me out yet."

"Do you have to go?" I ask, and then slap a hand over my lips. I shouldn't have asked that. His eyes are watching me, assessing, and I make a half-smile, half-grimace. "Sorry. I appreciate you being here. That's all. Thank you."

"It's my pleasure, sweetheart. Would you like me to come back tomorrow?"

I want to say yes. Because there is nothing familiar, in my world. There is only him. He is becoming a touchstone of familiar.

"If you'd like to," I answer, trying not to be demanding.

His head tilts to the side. "I'll make a deal with you, Peyton. If you will tell me something you learned about yourself—I'll come back. But you have to learn something. About who you are or who you were. Deal?"

I blink at him. Rike is staring at me, and there's a wild hope in his eyes. He wants me to do this. It matters.

And it's a helluva a lot better than trying dream therapy with an idiotic shrink.

"How do I tell you?"

A wide smile spreads across his face, and he pulls out a phone. "It's cheap. Just a prepaid thing. I programmed my number in here. I want you to text or call when you've figured it out. One thing, ok?"

"What if you're busy?"

His eyes darken, and my breath catches in my throat. "I won't be. I won't ever be too busy for you, Peyton."

I don't know what to say to that, so I just bob a quick nod and his tension eases a little. He hesitates, and then hands me a small, leather-bound book. "This was in your purse when you were brought in. I wanted you to have it."

I take it from him with numb fingers and he leans down, brushing a kiss over my hair. It takes everything in me to keep from shivering.

"I hope I see you tomorrow, Peyton," he murmurs. Then he walks to the door. Pauses there and grins over his shoulder at me. "Knock, knock."

A silly smile tugs my lips. "Who's there?"

"Cows go."

"Cows go who?"

He smirks. "Cows go moo, not who."

I giggle, and he winks at me, and then he's gone.

And I'm alone. With my thoughts and a tablet.

I could Google. I can't imagine I was a girl who didn't like social media. But I think using that to get a fact is cheating. The notebook is sitting in my lap, with the cell phone. It was mine. Why is that terrifying?

I take a deep breath and flip it open.

The pages are covered in neat, tiny script, looping little letters. I stare at it for a moment, my gaze skimming the page before I flip to the next. And the next. Page after page.

Poetry.

And it's gorgeous. I flip through the book slowly, reading the poetry. It's everything from Byron and Frost to people I've never heard of. I'm tempted to Google them, and I finally reach for my own notebook. Jot down a few things to look up tomorrow, before I settle into the pillows and read.

It's hours later when the nurse comes in to check my vitals. Her gaze tracks over me and the array of books and the open notebook. Her gaze brightens and she gives me a smile. "Remember anything, Peyton?"

I make a face and shake my head. She clucks softly. "The doctor is talking to your parents tomorrow."

I shift and straighten. "I would really prefer he didn't."

Her eyes widen, and I bite my tongue. Why the hell did I say that? I don't know. But the mere idea of him discussing my medical condition with my parents makes me want to crawl into a hole and hide from everyone. And fire him immediately.

"Please let him know I want to be consulted before he reaches out to anyone. I'm sure that I'm protected by privacy laws." I say it evenly, but I'm seething. Just because I've lost a chunk of my memory doesn't mean I don't remember basic privacy.

Her face goes white and she bobs a nod as she goes quiet and finishes taking my stats. Then she's gone and I'm left staring at the notebook of beautiful words, and the unshakable feeling that I don't—didn't—like my parents.

The why is a lot harder to figure out.

I pick up the phone and text quickly:

Peyton: *I know my one thing.*
Rike: *Tell me. Blow me away.*
Peyton: *Don't be pushy. You said one thing. Not blow-you-away revelations.*

I can hear him laughing even though he's not here. I grin, and tap out quickly.

Peyton: *I'll tell you tomorrow. Thanks for keeping me company tonight.*

I wait a moment for a response, but none comes. And I'm okay with that.

I lean back on the bed and lose myself in the words on the page, until my eyes are too heavy to stay open, and all I can see is beauty.

I fall asleep with two truths ringing in my mind.

I don't like my parents. And I absolutely adore poetry.

Before & After

Chapter 5: Before

Scotty is watching me from a barstool as I tap at the drums nervously. It's been two weeks since that first date in Keegan's record store, and I still haven't brought Peyton home. She's flirted, and we've done dinner, and constant texting. She still comes by to listen to us play, but she scooted out before I could talk to her last week, texting quickly that she had a class early the next morning.

Which might be true. It might be she doesn't want to get serious enough that she's meeting Scott

"You need to get laid," Scott says, and I flick him a dirty look.

"Have you even kissed her yet?" he asks, and I duck behind the drums. He barks out a startled laugh, half choking on his beer. "You haven't. Shit, bro, you're losing your touch."

"Shut the fuck up," I growl. "I'm not fucking this up because I'm horny."

Scott laughs again and I stand abruptly, glaring at my brother. Amused blue eyes meet mine, red hair framing a private smile that tells me I'm not in trouble, but I'm skating close to it.

Peyton reaches out and snags Scott's Redd's, sipping from it as she saunters up to the stage and climbs up. She's wearing a tight little jean skirt that rides up a little when she steps up, and I get the quick flash of her smooth thigh, the hint of bright blue panties before she's on the stage and stalking toward me.

She moves with a prowling grace that make me hard, and I swallow, watching as she closes in on me.

"You're horny and you won't touch me?" She murmurs, soft enough that even in the still quiet of the bar, only I hear her words. "I must be reading your signals wrong, Jokes. I thought you were in this."

Disappointment shimmers in her bright eyes, and I move without thinking. For once, the voices hissing that she's too good for me are silenced as I drag her into me. Her body is hot and soft under the jean skirt and a tight-fitting tank that caresses every fucking curve. I drop my head down, skimming along her skin as I murmur, "Sweetheart, I've gotten off every day for the past three months, thinking about your tight little body in my bed. Thinking about kissing you until you can't think and watching you fall apart while I'm buried in your perfect pussy."

She makes a tiny gasp against my ear and I lick a line across the curve of her neck and she shudders, her hand coming up to clutch my shoulders, nails digging in.

"You like that, don't you? That I've spent months hung up on you. That I've come all over myself thinking about you."

She whimpers and I swallow my smile as I pull back. Stare in her eyes as she struggles to breathe evenly. "How wet are you right now, Peyton?"

She licks her lips and my dick twitches. I swallow a groan as she comes up on tiptoes and leans in, her lips brushing against my ear as she whispers, "Fucking soaked."

I have her against me before I realize I moved, and her lips are against mine and it's every fucking thing I expected. Wanted. Fantasized about for months. Her hands are on my shoulders, nails digging in, and I fucking love it. I lick along the seam of her lips, my hand coming up and framing her face as the other finds her waist, the smooth band of skin between her skirt and her top. I catch her bottom lip, tugging softly, and her nails bite down as she gasps. I shift her, twisting and pushing her back until she hits the wall. One leg hitches up around mine and I groan as her tongue slides against mine and her skirt rides up between us.

I'm about a minute from dragging her into the back stockroom and fucking her against the cases of beer. She grabs my hand, and brings it between us as her leg drops. I pull back a hairsbreadth, startled, and her blue eyes are fierce and hot on mine as she guides my hand down the front of her skirt.

I'm too aware of the people behind us, and the girl in my arms, the way she's pushing me past every fucking boundary I know.

Then I feel her, her pussy smooth and soft and so, "Jesus, you're so fucking wet," I hiss, my fingers slipping through her folds. Her eyes are closed, and her mouth is slightly open, as she moves against me in the tiniest thrust, her clit rubbing against my palm.

It might be the most erotic thing I've ever seen.

"Rike," Scott yells, but he seems very far away. The bar is impossibly quiet, and she's shuddering in my arms. I twist, coming in front of her a little more, pushing her deeper into the shadows of the wall and my fingers sink into her.

I swallow my curse as her nails dig in again, pain flashing through me and slamming into my cock, and her lips open.

I kiss her, taking the scream as she spasms around my hand, wet heat and shuddering silky muscles and the scent of sunshine and sugar all around me as I drink down her screams and kiss her like I'm dying.

Slowly, slowly, she settles, her body relaxing against the wall, and I slip my hand from her skirt, straightening it.

I just finger-fucked Peyton in the middle of a bar. A not empty bar.

What the actual fuck is wrong with me?

She grabs me by the jaw as I step away from her and her eyes are furious and hot, and my mouth goes dry. "Don't you dare regret this, Jokes. Don't you fucking dare." She pushes past me before I can protest, before I can say anything, and I wait a second, trying to get my composure and to get my fucking hard-on to go down before I turn to face the entire room.

I feel someone at my back, and glance at Scotty.

"I got the room cleared," he says. "Before you guys went at it like fucking rabbits."

He grins, and I want to punch him for seeing that even as I'm glad he had the presence of mind to clear the room.

"I wasn't thinking," I mutter.

"No, but going without sex will fuck with anyone's head. And Siren looks like she was into it."

"Quit calling her that. Her name is Peyton."

He glances at her from the corner of his eye. Peyton is settling into her booth in the corner of the bar, opening her computer and going to work like I didn't just molest her onstage.

For the first time, my heartbeat settles.

She wanted it just as bad as I did.

"Of course she did, you fucktard. You might be horny but you don't fucking assault girls. Just keep that shit off the stage—we've got people coming in." He says, answering the thought I didn't realize I'd voiced.

I glance at him and nod. He point at the back bathroom and I follow his wordless directive.

It's tiny and stinks and I close the door behind me, leaning on it.

I can fucking smell her on my skin, and I groan.

Because I'm fucking hard. Again.

Chapter 6: After

I want to peel back

The cryptic smile and the

Quiet logic, the cynical amused

Faces that you show the world.

(Rike's poems to Peyton)

"I think I need to see her."

Rike glances at me. We're in the hospital cafeteria, sitting across from each other in a booth. He's been sketching for almost an hour while I journal. But I haven't really written anything. It's been over a week since I woke up, and my days have a pattern. Morning physical therapy and counseling. Texting with Rike. Afternoons spent playing card games and listening to ridiculous jokes while he stares at me with cloudy blue eyes that are full of secrets.

I wish I knew why he was here. I wish I didn't feel like he was hiding something from me. And I wish I was brave enough to demand to know what it was.

But I'm not. And fighting with my doctors and psychiatrist about my insistence to keep my family at a distance has been consuming me.

Rike looks distant, nibbling at his lip in a way that is way too fucking distracting.

"Who?"

"Lindsay," I say. "We came in together. Maybe I know her. It makes sense. And what if she's all alone like I am?"

His eyebrows go up. "I didn't think you were alone," he says.

I flush. "You know what I mean."

Rike sighs and put his pencil aside, giving me his full attention. "I do know what you mean but I need you to hear me. You aren't alone. I'm here. I'm not going away."

We sit in silence for a long moment staring at each other and then, "But I don't understand why," I say.

He smiles, that mysterious smile I adore and stands up, "You don't have to understand why. Come on. You're right: seeing her will do you some good."

He helps me into my wheelchair—the doctors want me in it until the casts come off my leg and arm—and tucks a blanket around me, always with that careful caution that I'm coming to expect.

He treats me with such reverent care, like a strong wind will shatter me. And it might. I know nothing about who I am—sometimes, it feels like he is all that holds me together.

I catch his hand as he straightens and his eyes flash to mine. Hungry and questioning and so intense it takes my breath away for a moment.

I want to kiss him. I don't know why, but I do, and I think he can see that desire my eyes. He leans into me, his forehead against mine. "You're making this so hard, Peyton," he murmurs.

"Sorry," I say faintly, and his lips twitch a little.

"No, you aren't."

I grin. I'm really not. I fucking love that I'm affecting him.

Rike sighs, and straightens. "Behave."

"You don't really want me to," I sass, and he barks a laugh as he pushes me through the cafeteria and into the halls of the hospital.

The playful mood slips away as we get closer to the ICU. I'm nervous, suddenly, as the doors swing open and the sterile environment stares back at me.

A nurse offers me and me—Rike, especially—a friendly smile, but he ignores it as he steers me deeper into the unit. Until we come to a stop at unit seventeen.

There is a steady beeping, the constant hum of machines, and it's comforting. It means life—maybe broken, but still life.

Rike pulls open the door and maneuvers me in deftly, and the door swings shut behind me.

I barely notice. My entire being is focused on the girl in the bed.

Her hair is chopped brutally short, almost shaved, and she's covered in bruises. She's wrapped in bandages, so fucking beat up I want to cry. "You didn't tell me it was this bad."

"You didn't need to know this, Peyton."

"That isn't your call," I say harshly. "You aren't part of my life. You don't even *know* me."

"Don't argue," a voice says. I startle. The movement jars my leg, and I hiss in pain as it slices into me, hot and searing.

Rike is by my side instantly, his hands catching mine, gentle. His voice is soothing, centering me, and it keeps me in the moment, focused on something other than the pain.

"Come on, Pey, breathe though it," he murmurs, and I gasp, tears stinging my eyes. Nod at him as he continues to murmur softly. It takes a few minutes, but when I can breathe again, he sits back on his heels and looks past my head, to whomever is standing behind me. "Don't fucking do that," he snarls, and I shiver. There is real anger there, a kind of bone deep dislike that I haven't seen from Rike before now, and it chills me.

I don't like this side of him.

"Then don't fucking disturb her," the other man snaps. His gaze skates over me, and I see the flash of fury in his gaze before his expression goes smooth and blank. "What are you doing here?"

"She wants to see Lindsay."

The other man snorts. "*Now* she does."

"Scott," Rike growls, and I finally shake myself.

"Can I have a few minutes alone with her? Please?"

They both stare at me for a moment and I force my chin up, a defiance I don't actually feel in the face of their anger that makes no sense.

But I was right. Seeing her helps. If only because it confirms what I knew.

"Please," I say again.

Scott huffs and stalks past me, throwing an order over his shoulder. "Don't fucking wake her up. She was up all night with the fucking nurses."

I wonder if he knows any curse words besides fuck.

"Shit. And damn. And hell. As in, I don't give a damn what the hell you want. Your shit doesn't concern me." He points at the bed. "She does. Don't fuck this up."

I flush, heat crawling in my cheeks, and he laughs as he walks out of the room. "At least that thinking out loud thing hasn't changed. "

I look at Rike, a searching stare, but he's ignoring me, stalking after Scott and letting the door swing close behind them.

And there is nothing but the girl sleeping in the bed to distract me.

I nudge myself closer to the bed, and stare at her.

I don't know her. Except—I do. I don't know who they are, these people, but I know them, or I knew them. And they don't fit who I imagine I was.

"What the hell were we doing? Why was I with you and where were we going?"

"I can't tell you."

She's staring at me and I didn't even realize she was awake. Her eyes are tired, glassy, a too dull brown, and sad. She winces as she shifts, twisting a little to stare at me.

Her words are sinking in, slowly. Too slowly. I narrow my eyes at her. "What do you mean, you can't?" I demand.

Her gaze darts past me for a minute and she licks her lips. A nervous habit.

How the hell do I know that's a nervous habit?

"Lindsay, what the fuck does that mean?"

"I promised, Peyton. I promised I'd let him do this his way. I—I can't tell you anything."

"Do I know you?" I demand, and lurch forward. Agony sings through me, but it's amazing what you can ignore when something else is at stake. Pain is fleeting—it'll be gone soon. My memory will stay gone, and she *knows* something.

"Who *am I?*"

She's sobbing, and I'm clutching her leg, shaking her. "I promised, Peyton. I can't. I'm so sorry."

"Who the hell would you promise that to?" I shout. "This is my life you're fucking playing games with!"

The door slams open and she breaks down, sobs shaking her as Scott shoves my wheelchair aside and cradles her against his chest.

"I told you to leave her the fuck alone."

"*She fucking knows me,*" I scream.

"Get her out of here, Rike," Scott yells, and the nurses are all around us. Lindsay's machines are going crazy, and I can feel Rike pulling me away from her, can hear the apologies he's almost shouting as we're all but thrown out of ICU, and I can hear Lindsay crying and Scott cursing, but it's all distant. A long way away. Muffled and distorted as I scream after her.

She knows me. She knows who I am, and where I come from. She knows it all. And the bitch won't tell me anything.

I feel a prick in my arm, and the world swims as icy heat flood my veins.

Rike is crouched in front of me, and I can see the apology in his eyes. He's murmuring and as the sedative the nurses gave me starts working, pulling me inexorably toward oblivion, I shape the words. Sift through them. *I'm so sorry, Fish.*

It doesn't make sense. Why is Rike sorry? Why is he here? What—my gaze widens and I grit out a curse. "Oh, you fucking *asshole.* It was you. You made her promise not to tell me anything."

Guilt floods his gaze and he looks away. And the darkness pulls me down, with the sound of his betrayal, and flaring alarms all that I can hear.

Chapter 7: Before

There are a few defining moments for every relationship. Shit where, afterwards, you know things have changed. Finger banging Peyton on a stage in a bar was one of those points.

When I was with her, I could forget for a few minutes that everything we were doing was stupid and doomed to fall apart. Because she was in my arms or holding my hand. But there was something that needed to happen that couldn't wait—a big fucking defining moment.

"I want to take you out," I say, softly. She's sitting next to me, her fingers flicking lazily through the stacks of records, and her gaze comes up to mine when I murmur those words. Curiosity is bright in her eyes and I swallow hard. This girl fucking undoes me. I don't know how or why, but she can unravel me completely with just a single smile, all sweet innocence and dirty promises.

"Where are we going?"

I let out a breath. "Scotty wants to get some new ink. You wanna come with us?"

She wrinkles her nose, an expression that I love on her pretty face. "You want me to go out with you and Scotty?"

I nod, and my breath stills.

She shrugs. "Ok."

That's it? Her gaze goes back to the stack of records, and some of the tension eases in my shoulders, relaxing some even as I frown at her. "You aren't going to argue with me?"

"Do you want me to?" she asks.

"Of course not," I say, annoyed for some reason. Her gaze snaps up, just a little bit warning, and I breathe out, trying to keep from snapping.

"Look, he's your best friend. I get it. There's something about him that's important to you. We've been seeing each other for almost a month. I'd be more concerned if you didn't want me to hang out with him." She shoves the records at me and stands, and I get a quick peek of pink lace panties as she straightens her rumpled skirt. "But if either of you think you're going to share me, you can get that shit out of your head. I get that you have in the past, but I'm not into him, and I'm not going to fuck him to keep you happy."

Without thinking, I catch her hand and drag her back down to the couch. Catch her lips with mine and swallow her startled little noise of surprise as my hands smooth down her luscious curves.

She comes to life under my hand, arching into my caress and almost purring as I lick into her mouth. Her teeth close over my lower lip, and I swallow my groan as she pulls away, pain flickering through me, chasing the high of kissing her.

"I won't fucking share you. Scotty gets a lot, but the most he'll get to participate is listening to you scream when I fuck you at our place. Because I know that when I strip you down, you'll be a screamer. Won't you, Pey?"

"If that's what you want," she whispers as my hand trails up her leg, and she shifts, her legs spreading a little in obvious invitation. "But you have to actually fuck me to find out."

"You want that. You want me to fuck you until you scream." I lick the shell of her ear and catch it with my teeth. "Does it turn you on that he'll listen to you, that he'll get off listening to me fuck you?" She whimpers and reaches for my hand and I twist, dumping her from my lap unceremoniously.

"Come on," I say, rising and adjusting my hard-on. She glares at me, shoving her hair out of her eyes and I grin.

"No one likes a tease," she says and I smirk, leaning down to brush her lips lightly.

"Maybe not. But you, sweet girl, like me."

She growls lightly and I slap her ass before steering her toward the door.

"We're going now?"

"You ok with that?"

She shrugs, nibbling at her lip nervously Something I didn't expect from her. "Hey," I say softly. "What's going on in that pretty little head of yours?"

"What if he doesn't like me?"

I hesitate. I could tell her that it wouldn't matter, but this girl knows me well enough to know better. She's picked up too quickly just how important Scotty is. She won't buy my bullshit and maybe that's what I adore about her.

She's so fucking different from every girl I've ever met.

"Why don't—" I say, catching her by the hand and lacing our fingers, drawing her into me "—we figure that out if it becomes a problem? And until then, we agree that neither of us will worry about it. Ok?"

She bites her lip, and my dick, still hard, twitches in my jean. I nod at the door, and nudge her slightly. "Let's go, sweetheart."

Chapter 8: After

Easy doesn't make the lonely
easier to bear, and less
Suffocating.
It simply is.
I've tried them both.
And I would rather,
Fight and laugh and puzzle
Through the riddles,
And all the not easy.
If it means being with you.
(Rike's poems to Peyton)

I'm leaving the hospital.

That's what they keep telling me. That I'm leaving, and I'll be going—where?

Rike keeps trying to come back, and I keep refusing to see him. He's not offering me anything and he's holding all the cards. The fucking bastard is holding my memory hostage. It's psychological warfare and I don't care how he might make me smile, how sweetly he treats me—nothing can excuse that. It's indefensible.

But there's nothing more that the hospital can do for me. I have money—plenty, according to the ATM I use with the debit cards I find in the purse the EMTs brought in with me. So I make a plan.

And when my doctor discharges me, two weeks after I wake up with no memories and a shattered leg, I wheel myself out of the hospital. Alone. I think, very briefly, about going to see Lindsay before I leave, but the truth is I'm not sure what the point would be. She's got her own set of problems, recovering from the internal organ damage and the broken bones. They've moved her from ICU, but no one is even starting to talk about her going home. It's completely quiet on that front, and I've asked.

I think something is going on with her that no one wants to let me in on. Because I'm so fucking fragile. I huff a breath at the thought.

I *hate* being weak.

It takes the better part of two hours to get myself to a hotel, and settled in. It's not terribly nice.

As much as I have in my bank account, eventually it'll dry up, and I'm pretty sure that whatever job I might have had is long gone. So this little nest egg will have to last until I can find a new one or remember who the hell I am.

The hotel doesn't have a bellhop, but there is a big black man from maintenance sitting behind the counter, and he offers to help me carry my stuff up to my room. There isn't much—three bags from the hospital with meds and clothes, a bloody purse that came in from the accident, and the stuff that Rike brought to me. Which I should get rid of. I've tried to, a few times. I almost left the bag of his gifts on the bed when I left, but at the last second, I chickened out. I'm furious and I don't think I'll ever forgive him, but I also can't seem to bring myself to break ties completely.

I'm clearly an idiot.

"You shouldn't be here alone, ma'am," the guy rumbles at me as we take the elevator up to the third floor. I glance at him, and he's staring at his feet. The man is a giant, but he's got a shy gentleness about him that sets me at ease.

"Why?"

"Dangerous. And you're a lady," he adds, flushing a darker shade of brown.

I glance away to hide my smile, and shrug. "Beggars and choosers. You know the drill," I say.

"What happened?" he asks, nudging the wheelchair.

"Car accident. It left me a scrambled memory—I'm trying to put the pieces back together."

He frowns thoughtfully but doesn't say anything else as he pushes my wheelchair off the elevator when the doors slide open. I sit quiet while he opens the door to my room and wheels me in, laying my bags across the bed. Without giving me a chance to say anything, he crosses to the desk and scribbles on the pad of paper there. Taps it with his pen while giving me a serious look.

"I'm Tommy. I work here to fill my time—since my wife died, I don't like being home alone. You need anything at all—food or a ride to the store or help downstairs. You call me. I'm here every day but Sunday." He says sternly. I nod quietly and his gaze, so very fierce, gentles into the concern that looks like what I imagine my father would look like, if he could be bothered to care. "You should not be here, alone. I will help, if you'll let me."

"Thank you," I whisper, and he grins. Bobs his head at me and ducks out the door. I let out a breath and stare around the little room.

A TV. Two beds. Three bags. A view of a city I've never been to, and that I live in.

A cell phone that has been silenced, blinking with unread messages.

It's not much to build a life on. Not nearly enough.

I shove that thought aside and work on getting out of the wheelchair, and on to the bed.

I don't know who I am. Rike holds the keys to everything, but he's not giving them up and I'm not going to wait for him to tell me. So it's time to research.

***

I'm lost in Facebook when I hear a tap on the door. My head jerks up and then, muffled, I hear Tommy calling to me. "Ma'am?"

Relief sags my shoulders. "Hang on," I yell. It takes a few minutes, but I make it to the door and pull it open.

Tommy is standing there with a bag of food and a hopeful look. "You hungry?

I tilt my head. "Tommy you don't have to take care of me. I'm ok."

He hesitates, some of the light in his going out. "Sorry. I—you remind me of my wife. She was stubborn and brave. I didn't mean to be pushy."

"How long ago did she pass away?" I ask, softly.

Grief flickers in his eyes, "Four years ago. They said it'll get easier, but it doesn't. It just gets familiar."

"Peyton. My name is Peyton," I say. "And I am hungry. I was working." He glances over the bed, at the little notepad that I've scribbled on and ripped apart, the notebook that's spread out with names and lines crisscrossing like a fucked up map.

"Well, eat something. And try to get some sleep tonight," he says.

I nod and take the bag. "Thank you."

"Need me to bring you anything in the morning?"

I shake my head and he wilts but doesn't push. Just gives me a quick smile before he ducks out. "Lock up behind me," he advises and then he's gone.

I do.

It begins a routine that quickly becomes comfortable. He comes by in the morning with breakfast and whatever random thing he thinks I need. And in the evening, when his shift is ending, he comes by again with dinner. Sometimes he stays and we talk about the hotel and what he did during the day. He learns quickly that I don't like questions and stops asking after a few days. But he's a constant presence, with stories about his wife, and the forty years they spent together before cancer ripped apart their happy life.

It still bugs me when I call him for the first time.

"Tommy? It's Peyton, in 337." I hesitate and he laughs.

"I only know the one Peyton," he teases. "Now what do you need?"

"Do you think you could help me downstairs? I have appointments at the hospital all day—"

"I'll be right down. Get your stuff together."

He hangs up before I get the "thank you" out of my mouth and I let out a little sigh.

When Tommy knocks on the door five minutes later, I'm ready and vaguely nervous. I've got more information about the retrograde amnesia, and about myself.

But knowing that I'm the daughter of a politician from Tennessee, that I hate my family and spent a good chunk of my high school years in and out of rehab—none of that tells me why I'm living in Austin or who the hell Rike is to me.

And it should have come back by now. That's the part that bothers me the most. That my memory is still gone.

"You're quiet today, Peyton," Tommy observes.

"Do you think, that if a person doesn't remember where they came from, they're still bound by the decisions that they made before?" Tommy throws me a startled look and I wave a hand dismissively. "Never mind."

"Is that what's wrong? That you can't remember?"

We've talked, briefly and vaguely, about my accident. He knows something is wrong, and sometimes, when he's talking about a movie he's watched recently, I stare at him with a blankness that is frightening.

I stare at the city we're driving through. I feel a strange longing for it, even as I find it too big and too foreign. It's not Nashville. Not Sweet Water. I miss my quiet, backwater little town in the middle of nowhere Tennessee.

"Yes," I whisper.

"Peyton, no one gets to decide who you are but you. Even if you had your memories."

I think of Rike, and how easy it is to be with him. How present he is, even when we were both lost in our own worlds.

How fucking happy I was.

I'm so tired of thinking about him, of being pulled into feelings I don't know what to do with, and that stupid fucking feeling of loss.

I can't mourn losing someone I never had. And maybe, before was different. But Rike was never mine. Not the me I am today.

I let the thought roll around my head as Tommy pulls into the visitor bay at St. David's. There's a line of cars waiting and I sit quietly, waiting as he inches forward until he finally puts the truck in park and hops out, tugging my wheelchair down before he helps me out and helps me into it, stepping back and letting me situate myself. When I nod at him, he grabs my black purse—a new purse, one he brought to me on the third morning at the hotel—and wheels me to the sidewalk. "I'm going to park, and I'll take you in," he says.

"Tommy, you don't have to do that," I say, but he's already jogged away, sliding into the truck and pulling away to park. He's going to be in trouble if he stays with me. They'll miss him at the hotel.

"Peyton."

I jerk and look around. The voice is vaguely familiar, and it clicks suddenly when I see Scott. He's walking toward me, smoking.

He looks like shit, exhaustion clear on his face even under the oversized sunglasses and ball cap. He's hunched forward, almost hiding. "God, where the fuck have you been?" he breathes, leaning down and hugging me.

I'm stiff in his arms, and he seems to realize it, because he pulls back and stares at me.

"Holy fuck. You don't know, do you? You still don't know who we are."

"Feel free to clue me in," I snap.

He takes off his ball cap and ruffles his hair, a scowl lining his forehead. "I'm going to fucking kick his ass." Scott crouches. "This wasn't the deal. We wouldn't have agreed if we knew it was going to take this long for him to come clean about shit. I'll talk to him."

"Don't," I say, and his face goes pale. "I don't know who or what I was to you or Lindsay. I don't know what Rike is playing at. And I don't fucking care."

"Peyton, you don't mean that," he protests.

"I do. I'm not that girl. I don't even fucking remember that girl. So if he wants to play god with someone's life and memories, he'll have to find someone else because I'm done."

"What are you going to do?"

It's a good question. I refuse to go to my parents. That bridge isn't quite burned, but I'd set fire to it before I crossed it.

"It's not your concern," I say.

"You're my girlfriend's best friend, and you're Rike's—" He stops, and I lean forward.

"I'm what? What the hell am I to him?"

He shrugs. "You're his. You think you can walk away, and he might even let you, for a time.

Because he's a dumbass. But it won't stick, Peyton. Rike doesn't know how to be without you."

I smile, so cold it hurts even me. "He'll have to fucking figure it out."

"Peyton?"

Scott tenses, and his gaze darts to Tommy. Back to me, questioning.

"Pey, is he bothering you?" Tommy asks. He sounds cold. Threatening, for the first time since I've met him, and Scott straightens slowly.

"Dude, she's practically family," he says. As if it were true, and an excuse. It's neither.

"We're going to be late," I say and Tommy's pushing me forward.

"You're really just going to leave. Let this random dude into your life, and ignore your family? Is that it?"

"My family?" I bark. "Are you fucking insane? Because keeping shit like *who I am* from me isn't what family does. Fuck you, Scott."

Tommy pushes me forward, another two steps.

"Lindsay is paralyzed. She won't ever fucking walk again, Peyton. And she needs her best friend. You don't want me or Rike—ok. But she needs you."

I glance back at him, and I know he's telling the truth.

"I'm sorry," I whisper. "I really am. But I need to figure out who I am and what the hell I'm doing. I can't be strong for someone else if I can't even figure out where I belong."

He gives me a sad smile. "You belong with us, Peyton. You always have."

***

Tommy is quiet the entire way home, after my appointments end. He gets me back to my hotel room, and I curl up on the bed. The doctor had nothing helpful to say, and no clue why I haven't remembered anything. She's ordered new scans of my brain, but what the hell will that do?

I'm so tired I can't even think, and Scott's words are still running in my head, an endless loop that keeps mocking me.

"Why are you walking away from them?" Tommy asks, pulling chocolate milk from my mini fridge and pouring a cup. He's watching me as he settles into his chair and sips it thoughtfully. Waiting for an answer I don't have.

I'm quiet for a long time, thinking about it, and he finally stands. "Don't push away people who care about you because they did something out of misguided good intentions. My Luce did that once, a few years after we married. It was right after we found we couldn't have children. She thought I should find someone who could give me children. Almost destroyed us." His dark, old eyes find mine, and I can see the sadness there still. "Don't throw away a life you've built because you're scared and can't remember building it. You come from good things and good places, and that guy, he cared about you. Maybe it's okay to think about that. To care about it too."

"They know who I am and they're not telling me."

"But maybe Rike has a reason for it. Maybe you should listen to his reason." He hesitates. "What do you have to lose, Peyton?"

I think about it for a long time, when he's gone. Until my eyes are drooping closed.

Nothing. I have nothing left to lose.

Chapter 9: Before

The tattoo shop has become one of her favorite places. Which makes me irrationally happy. She's becoming a fixture in my life. Her flame red hair brightens my view from the stage on Thursday and most Fridays, and she shows up at Keegan's unexpectedly—the old bastard even warms up to her when she stops by and chats with him before she drifts to me and snuggles into my side.

But for all that we're together (for all intents and purposes), she's keeping part of herself wrapped in secrets and dodges my questions. There's so much she doesn't say—questions she dodges and slides away from, a past that she doesn't want to share with me.

She's balancing cross-legged on a stool at the bar while Scotty and I finish the setup and I glance at her, her eyes distant as she taps away on that damn computer.

"What is she working on?"

I shrug.

"You don't know?" Scotty demands, his voice startled.

I give him the flat warning glare that usually manages to shut him up, but he just shakes his head, laughing. "Ask her."

"Tried that," I grunt. He huffs, a quiet noise of displeasure, and I nod.

"Are we playing the new song?" He asks.

I hesitate. I don't usually sing. I prefer to be in the background, playing drums while Scott plays rock god. It's where I'm comfortable--I've never wanted to be a rock star. I just want to create shit.

But occasionally, I'll write something that is too personal and he'll insist. I glance at where she's perched at the bar in a gravity-defying contortion as she works on something she won't share.

"Let's play it by ear," I say simply and he grunts in acknowledgement. "Can you finish this?" An eyebrow arches but he nods and I slap him on the back before I jog across the bar to where she's sitting.

I come up behind her, slipping my arms around her waist and pressing a kiss to the curve of her neck. I inhale the scent of her and get a quick peek at the computer screen, the words blurring as she closes it quickly and turns in my arm, her lips lifting up and finding mine. I smile against her as her fingers dig into my scalp and she shivers a little as I lick across her lips before pulling back.

"What do monkeys wear when they cook?"

Her eyes brighten and one corner of her lips hooks up into a grin. "I don't know. What?"

"An ape-ron." I deadpan and she laughs.

I lean in and steal another kiss, desperate for the taste of her laugh.

Peyton always tastes sweet and light, almost addictive, but when she's laughing, it's more than that—it's like drinking down sunshine, and I can't resist that. She sighs a little and I swallow my groan as I pull away from her, licking my lips to catch the last bit of her taste.

"Are you staying for the whole set?" I ask huskily.

She shrugs, her shoulders bare and delicate above a little tank top that makes me itch to pull it off of her. "Depends on how adoring your fans get."

I bite down on the acidic response that wants to rise. I haven't touched a girl—haven't even looked at one—since before that first night that I talked to her. It's been hell to listen to Scott fucking girls at the loft while I sat with my hard-on and fantasies of her lips around me. But I hadn't touched them and I hadn't pushed her for the more I knew she'd willingly give. Because there were too many secrets between us still.

"What are you working on?" I ask abruptly and her eye widen. Shutter. Block me out, and even though I expect it, it still fucking hurts.

She sees it and reaches for me. "Jokes."

I pull back and shake my head. "This won't work if we refuse to trust each other," I say and her eyes flare with hurt and denial. I hate seeing that look in her eyes. But I bite back the apology and step back, toward the stage.

I want her to stop me. To explain. She doesn't, and with a sigh, I return to Scott. Slip behind my drum set and sprawl on the stool. "I need to get fucked," I grit out.

His eyes widen, and I know what he's thinking. That it's a bad idea, that I'll hate myself for it later, that I'm self-sabotaging.

But he doesn't say any of those things. He just nods at me and kicks off the set, and I follow him on the drums.

And I know that a pretty girl who looks nothing like Peyton will fall asleep in my bed tonight, after my best friend and I fuck her for hours.

If I know him at all, he's already picked her.

Chapter 10: After

I want to drown myself in you,
consume your soul,
until there is no you. no me.
only us.
(Rike's poems to Peyton)

The phone is sitting on the table in front of me, and I twitch, smoothing my pants down. Again. I should have set this up for anywhere but here. It occurs to me now, when it's too late to do anything to fix it.

I let out an unsteady breath and push my hair back. Stare at the phone. He hasn't called to cancel, so I have to assume he's coming.

I almost scream when the knock on the door comes, even though I'm expecting it. Waiting on it. It still startles me. I shift and wheel my chair to the door and pull it open.

Rike is standing there, and for just a moment we stare at each other. His eyes are desperate and alive with hunger, raking over me.

When Rike looks at me, it's not just seeing. He devours me with his gaze, claiming every inch of me, a familiarity that hasn't made sense. It does now, and I feel the press of his gaze on my bare toes, up over my legs and still healing body, lingering a moment on my breasts, and finally, coming to meet my own gaze. It's invasive, like a touch, and I want to be bothered by it more than I am. I want to slap him into submission, want to remind him that I'm not his to look at that way. But instead, I flush, and almost purr, blossoming under the scrutiny.

"Come in," I say, and he takes a step into the room. If I were standing, we'd be pressed against each other. As it is, I'm left craning my head back to stare at something other than his crotch. I scoot my wheelchair back, retreating to the far bed, where I sleep.

He's quiet while I maneuver from the chair to the bed. "Do you want anything? I've got some beer in the fridge."

Rike's eyebrows climb and I shrug. "I don't like it very much, but Tommy brings random shit by."

His features cloud. "You love beer," he says.

I blink at him. I haven't had a beer in years. Since high school. And I hated it.

"Who is Tommy?" he asks.

"A friend. He's been helping me while I stay here—I'm not incredibly mobile with that thing," I say. He nods. I could add more—explain more—but frankly I don't think he deserves it.

"Scott and Lindsay both say you know me. *They* know me. And neither of them are telling me shit, because you won't let them."

"I have my reasons, Peyton. I need you to trust them."

"I can't," I say. "I don't know you." He flinches and I point at him. "And see that. Right there.

That tells me I should and that you aren't willing to tell my how or why. You do realize how fucked up this is, don't you?"

He's quiet, staring at me.

I want to sketch that look. Because it's stealing my breath and breaking my heart.

"I'm trying, sweetheart," he whispers. "I need you to work with me."

"I want to," I confess, and his gaze darts to mine. "This is terrifying. Not knowing anything—I want to know. I want to trust that you do and you're doing this for a reason. But I don't know you. And I need a reason to trust you. You want me to work with you. But you're holding all the cards, and I need you to give just a little."

He exhales heavily and shifts. I tense and he goes still. "Can I hold you? For just a minute?"

"Why?"

"Because I miss holding you. Because seeing you and not being able to touch you is killing me. Because I don't want to say this."

I nod and relief brightens his features as he pushes off the wall and comes to sit next to me. Not content, he reclines against the bed, and pulls me down next to him, arranging me to fit against him. One arm props under my head, and the other wraps around my waist, his fingers playing on the skin exposed under my tank top.

I can feel him, pressed against me at all points, his scent washing over me, and his lips on my hair.

And it feels so fucking right. Tears sting my eyes.

"I met you three years ago," he says. "You were in my bar, and I was playing the drums. And I think I loved you before we ever spoke."

""We were in love?" I ask.

He laughs, but the noise sounds broken. Almost sick. "Yeah, baby. We were. You were my whole world."

"And Scott and Lindsay?"

"My best friend, and you were rooming with Lindsay when we met. She actually brought you to the bar that first time, and you stayed."

My nose wrinkles and I twitch my shoulders. "Why? I hate bars."

"You liked to write there, while we played. Said it was inspiration."

I roll that over in my mind, playing with it. I don't know what to think of this. Of him. I can't deny that I'm drawn to him, that everything about him sets me at ease, but there is the simple truth: Rike, with his rough hands and too long beard, and tattoos tracing over his arms and neck—Rike isn't the kind of guy I've ever been attracted to.

"Talk to me, Pey," he says softly, his grip on me tightening just a little.

I shrug. "I don't know what to say. This is so—it's a lot, Rike. A lot to swallow and understand."

"I know that."

"Why didn't you tell me when I woke up?"

"Because who you are doesn't hinge on who loves you," he answers.

I twist to look at him, searching his face. "What if I choose that the person I am doesn't love you?"

I feel the flinch move through him, shaking him as he pulls me closer. His grip is so tight now, so desperate that it hurts. But I don't complain. I just burrow closer. Because if I walk away from him, I will not have this again, and I can't deny that the thought of that is enough to make tears swim in my eyes.

"If you need to be someone who isn't with me, I'll let you go, Peyton. I'll fucking hate it. But I've never wanted to keep you caged, and I won't be that guy now. I love you, and I want you in my life. Scott and Lindsay want you in our life. She needs you. But

I want you to be happy, with or without us. And I'll watch you walk away, if that is what you need for your happiness."

"I'm scared," I whisper. "I want to hide in you and let you take care of me. This—" I meet his gaze"—feels right."

Tension fills him. "But?"

"But...if I do, I'll never figure out who I was. What I loved or why. Who I was outside of the girl who loved you. And I need to know that, Rike."

Pain tightens his expression for a moment, and he blinks it away. "I can't help you?"

I hesitate, the offer so fucking tempting. And his gaze, so hopeful. "Rike," I whisper, and his gaze flares.

"Peyton, don't hate me," he murmurs, and then he's kissing me.

His lips are gentle, and the scruff of his beard is sharply abrasive as it brushes against my skin. His teeth nip at my lower lip, and I whimper. He groans and shifts, pulling me with him as he lays back. A big hand comes up to lace into my hair, holding me still as he kisses me, his tongue tangling with mine, retreating and thrusting back. His other hand is on my hip, cradling it and pulling me closer.

I groan, breaking the kiss as his erection nestles between my thighs, and I grind down against him.

Rike curses, and his lips are against my throat, warm wet kisses and soft, dirty words. I flush. What the hell. I don't do this.

His hand on my hip slips lower, over my ass, and I startle, going stiff in his arms.

And just that quickly, the moment is over. He sits up, and shoves his long hair back as I shift off of him. Sit awkwardly a few inches away.

Too fucking aware of his still-hard dick and how amazing it felt between my legs.

I'm so wet I'm almost squirming in my seat, and he's watching me with hooded, dark eyes. A smirk tugs his lips.

"I won't touch you without you asking, Peyton. But I want you to remember something. When I leave and you sink your fingers into that creamy wet pussy—I know. I know what you taste like. I know how you feel, and how you look so fucking gorgeous when you come. I know what you sound like when you scream. And I'll get off tonight, thinking about you here."

I stare at him, and I can feel the hot flush in my cheeks, and he smiles. Leans down and kisses me.

And then he stands, adjusts his dick, and leaves me alone.

***

I don't sleep well that night, or the next two nights. I'm horny and I want to get myself off—but after that first night, when I did come against my fingers, with his words playing through my head, the orgasm left me reeling, my head spinning and body shuddering. It was hot and sexy and dirty.

In the morning, a text had been on my phone.

Rike: *Did you wait until you were in bed before you got yourself off, or did you do it as soon as I left?*

I stared at it for a long time, and almost cursed when the second one popped up, the phone vibrating in my hand.

Rike: *I got off before I left the parking lot. And again in the shower, picturing you on your knees and my dick in your pretty mouth.*

I turn the phone off before I get another message, and spend the day reading a book and trying to ignore how horny I am.

The problem is, I'm not getting anywhere. And I know that there is a nearby source of information.

Tommy has been coming by, like clockwork, and he nudges my barefoot with his while I eat dinner two nights later. "When you gonna see Rike again?"

I shrug. "I don't know. I have an appointment tomorrow for my cast to come off. I was thinking I should probably see Lindsay while I'm there."

"She's still in the hospital?" he asks, his eyebrows hitching upward.

I nod. "I can't take you to the hospital tomorrow," he says, and I tense. I knew better than to assume he would. But I did it anyway. Tommy has been as reliable as the sunrise, but I've been here now for almost two weeks and he has to be getting tired of babysitting me.

"I'll figure it out," I say.

He taps the phone sitting on my side table. "Call him. He'll take you."

"You really are in his corner, aren't you?"

"I'm in the corner that gets you healthy and whole, Peyton. And he's part of that, even if you don't want to admit it yet."

"He's not my type."

"He is. Maybe he's not the type you think should be your type, but he's who you chose. And you hated that life anyway. Don't cling to your preconceived notions of who you think you should be because it's all you know. Be the girl you want to be for the rest of your life."

I consider that for a long time after Tommy leaves me alone, and eventually I turn on the phone.

The damn thing lights up with text messages and I flush, imagining how dirty and provocative they'll be.

I'm under no delusions that Rike has decided to leave me alone because I'm being quiet.

I ignore the messages, and pull up his number, dialing before I can chicken out.

"Peyton?" he says, and I can hear the surprise in his voice.

"Hi. Sorry. I don't mean to bother you, but—"

"You aren't. You will never be a bother. I thought we'd already gone over that."

I flush. "Um. Do you think you could give me a ride to the hospital tomorrow? My cast is coming off and Tommy can't take me. I think he got in trouble last week. But if you can't, I totally get it; I can get a cab to pick me up."

"What time?"

"Eleven. My appointment shouldn't take long, but I wanted to stop in and see Lindsay. If you have the time?"

"Of course," he says immediately. A tiny weight slides off my chest and I can breathe easier.

"Do you want to grab lunch, after?"

And just like that it's back.

"I don't know if that's a good idea," I say softly.

"I was your friend, long before you realized we were together, before. Let me be your friend, Peyton. You could use a friend."

"I need a friend who doesn't send me dirty texts," I say tartly.

He laughs, completely unrepentant.

"Fine. Lunch. But nothing fancy."

A secret smile colors his voice when he says, "Deal."

We're silent for a moment, and I can hear the sound of someone in the background calling his name, and I flush. "I should let you go."

"Yeah. I left a client in the middle of a tattoo piece. I should probably finish. But I'll see you tomorrow, perfect girl."

I hang up the phone, and turn it off. Because as much as I want to look at the texts I know it's a bad idea.

But I can't keep the smile off my face.

Tomorrow, I'm going to see him again.

Chapter 11: Before

I'm not sure what hurts more—my back or my head. It's pounding and my back feels like I brawled with Scott. I glance down and mutter a curse.

I groan and roll to my stomach, propping my head in my hand as the world spins dizzily.

"Scott," I croak.

"He went to get breakfast. Said to let you sleep."

I jerk upright, and glare over my shoulder at the blonde girl leaning against the door jam.

"What the hell are you doing here?"

Lindsay lifts one eyebrow, a quiet censure in that single move, and I am suddenly acutely aware that I'm naked in a room that doesn't belong to me.

"What happened?" I demand.

"You were drunk, Rike, but I didn't think you were that out of it," she says stiffly. I flip her off weakly and she makes a grumpy noise before retreating. I scramble to find some clothes in her absence, and tug on my jeans.

I hear a door slam, and for a moment, I think she's gone before I hear Scott talking to her, his voice pitched low. Then he appears, and his eyes skim over me, assessing.

"What happened?" I ask. I haven't been blackout drunk since the night—I shut that thought down and focus on my best friend. "Did I fuck her?"

Scott's expression turns grumpy. "You're a self-destructive bastard, you know that?"

I stare at him.

"You wanted to do this. Remember? You wanted to get laid and get Peyton out of your head." His voice is mocking and angry.

I do remember. But the thought of anyone…it makes my stomach twist and I want to shower that dirty feeling away. A look of disgust flicks across Scott's face and he steps into the room, crowding into me. "You're being a dick, man. I know shit with Peyton is messed up, but there's no reason to drag another girl into it. Especially a girl like Lindsay."

My eyebrows climb. "Lindsay is a one night stand that keeps coming back. What the hell does she have to do with anything?"

Scotty makes a disgusted noise and turns away. "You called her a whore, man. And then passed out naked in my bed. I'd be careful who you throw stones at when you're trying to cheat."

I flinch but he doesn't see and he wouldn't care.

Scotty doesn't like when we treat the girls like they're disposable. It's one thing to take a pretty

willing thing back home for fun. It's something else
to treat them like trash.

"I asked her because I knew she wouldn't go
through with it. She wouldn't let you fuck her. So
even if you didn't get your head out of your ass, you
wouldn't destroy the only good thing you've got
going for you," Scott says. "You're welcome."

I flinch. What the fuck was I doing last night?

No answers to be found in bed and I'm not
quite ready to face either of them. So I do what any
self-respecting dude would do and I duck into the
shower.

When I emerge, I feel vaguely human. My
head is still pounding and my stomach twists with the
remnants of too much beer the night before. Or
whatever we were drinking. I dress silently and then
step out of the bedroom and come face-to-face with
Scotty and Lindsay.

I manage, barely, to keep from making a face
at the sight of her.

"Coffee?" she says, her voice false warmth. I grunt and she moves to pour a cup, shooting Scotty a dark look while she does.

"Someone want to clue me in on what the hell happened last night?" I grit out.

Scotty lets out a slow breath. "You wanted a girl. I don't know what happened between you and the siren, but we started the set and you drank yourself fucking stupid. Lindsay and I got you home and I knew you what you said—but when she tried to touch you, you flipped the fuck out. Almost hit her."

His tone is dark and furious and I understand it. I've never touched a woman. Not in violence. That I was that shitty… "I'm sorry," I whisper. There's a breath of silence, and I stare at the dark coffee swirling in my mug. I don't want to see the disappointment in Scott's eyes and I'm not ready to look at Lindsay, not yet. "I don't know what else to say. Just that I fucked up and I'm so sorry. It's won't happen again."

"Do you even understand why it happened this time?" Lindsay asks, and her voice is tinged with annoyance.

"Because you aren't Peyton."

"You fucking knew that, Rike. You weren't under any illusions about who you were going home with."

I wasn't but I don't like what that says about me. "Why the fuck were you about to cheat on her?" she asks. "Even if I wouldn't have let it happen—what the fuck were you thinking?"

"It's not your business," I say, my gaze finally lifting to find hers.

"Bullshit. If you want that, you should probably avoid bringing me home. But here I am, and I got to deal with your shitty temper, so why don't you do us both the favor of being honest?"

"I was pissed. I don't know. It was a shit move and I won't repeat it."

She sits in silence for a moment, and I want to shove away from the table and bolt. Her gaze is too sharp and too assessing, and she doesn't like what she sees.

I don't blame her. I don't like me very much at the moment either.

"She cares about you, Rike. I know you're probably wondering, because I know Peyton. She likes her privacy and she fucking adores her secrets. But she likes you and she's let you get close to her. She doesn't do that for anyone. Don't fuck that up. And don't use me to hurt her. I'm not down with that bullshit."

My gaze cools and it skates over her, just as judgmental as hers on me had been. "Then what the fuck are you doing here?"

She shrugs. "I'm here for Scott, asshole. It has nothing to do with you."

I jerk, throwing a startled look at Scotty. He's ignoring me, sipping his coffee with a careful eye watching Lindsay.

What the hell is happening here, and how did I miss it?

"If you got your head out of your ass," Lindsay says, "maybe you wouldn't miss it."

Scott snorts a laugh and I realize I've spoken out loud. I flush.

"I'm gonna go," Lindsay says. Scott rises and kisses her briefly, and my eyes narrow. "Call me later?"

He nods and she waves at me with a narrowed eyed look before ducking out of the kitchen. I hear the apartment door slam behind her and my eyes go wide as I stare at my best friend like I've never seen him.

"What the actual fuck, Scott?"

He shrugs. "She's a nice girl, man. And we've both been bored, with you and Pey so wrapped up in each other."

I stare at him for a long minute, long enough that he fidgets and finally looks up at me.

His eyes are bright and daring me to say something. And because I'm an idiot, I do. "You actually care about Lindsay?"

"Why the hell is that so hard to believe?" he asks.

"Because that's not your M.O."

"Taking a month to fuck a girl isn't yours," he snaps back. And stands. Rinses his cup with his back to me.

It's covered in tattoos and scars, and I know all of the markings as well as I know my own hands. Fuck, I put some of them there. "She matters, Rike. End of story. Go back to your siren, and try not to fuck up what we both have going on here."

He doesn't say anything else as he stalks out of the kitchen and I'm left standing with a cold cup of coffee and no fucking clue how the hell our life got so weird so damn fast.

**

She's furious when I step into the little deli. It's off the campus of UT, cheap and not very good, but she likes it and I humor her. Right now, she's sitting in our normal booth, her computer on the table next to her BLT, ignored as she taps angrily at the phone in her hand.

Her gaze, when it swings up to meet mine, is hot and hurt, her lips a tight unforgiving line, and I let out an inaudible sigh.

"What the hell were you thinking last night?" she snaps while I slip into the booth.

"Why do psychologist hate elevators?" I stare at her, my gaze pleading for her to pick up her line of the joke, but she just sits back and crosses her arms over her pretty breasts, glaring and waiting for the explanation I don't have. "Because they drive you up a wall."

It doesn't get a response, but I didn't really think it would. I just had to try.

"I'm not in the mood for that shit, Jokes," she says sharply. "You fucking took my roommate home last night. How the hell do you expect me to overlook that?"

"I didn't know Peyton was your roommate," I say softly."

Her eyes go impossibly wide. "Is that really what you're worried about right now?"

"I think it is," I say slowly, deliberately, weighing my words. My gaze flicks over her face. "I think it's the issue. I know all the reasons we shouldn't work. I'm not good for you. I have a shit ton of baggage. I deal with shit by avoiding it, or picking a fight. By taking another girl home to fuck. Those are all the reasons we shouldn't work. But that's not the reason we'll fall apart."

"No?" she says sarcastically and I shake my head, leaning back. I'm mirroring her, and it pisses her off--her arms drop almost defiantly to the table top.

"It won't work because you refuse to trust me. You won't tell me a goddamn thing about you. You don't mind seeing my world—"

"What, a shitty bar and a record store? A tattoo shop? That's the only part of your world that you'll show me."

"That's the only part of my world that matters," I almost shout. "That's what I give a fuck about. So you can think it's shit. I don't give a fuck. But that's the reality of my world. A dirty bar, a shitty record store and a rundown tattoo shop. A best friend who doesn't know what the fuck boundaries are. That's what's important to me. The question is if you can deal with it."

"What the hell makes you think I can't?" she growls.

"Because you bolt every time things start to get serious." I shoot back. "You like the danger of it. You like me finger fucking you on the stage, you like that I'm not like all the other frat boys you play with.

But you won't be honest with me for five fucking minutes."

She's pale and almost shaking in her side of the booth, her fingers white-knuckled as they clench around her glass of unsweet tea. "I'm honest," she whispers. "I've never lied to you."

I shrug. "There's a helluva difference between lying and not telling the truth. What is it about me that you want but can't stand to get close to? Because that shit won't work for me."

"I'm not the one who took another dude home. You took my roommate home and fucked her and you're making it seem like I'm the one who fucked up."

"You don't trust me. So arguing with you about what happened isn't worth it."

I lean across the table and grab half her sandwich. She's staring at me and her eyes are furious. I sigh. "I didn't touch her. You can ask her and Scott if you don't believe me. Or you can tell me to fuck off and we can both cut our losses. Kinda wonder if that's not a good option."

"How can you say that?" she asks, hurt crossing her face, scrunching her brow and shadowing her blue eyes.

I shrug. "I know why this shouldn't work. I knew before I ever walked up to you in Barrie's. But I don't give a fuck. I'm falling for you. And I want to think you're falling for me. But you can't even tell me why you're in my bar or what the hell it is you do on that fucking computer. I find out after three weeks that the girl I fucked two months ago is your roommate. I can't do this. I can't fall for you if you're going to pull away from me and keep secrets. Because I won't be able to put up with them forever and eventually, I'll want to know some shit you aren't willing to share. And by then, I'll be in too deep." I look at her, and shrug. Smile a tiny little smile. "If this thing doesn't work, I'd rather it fall apart now."

I slip out of the booth. She's still staring at me, her eyes wide and terrified. Why the hell does she look so scared? I shove that thought aside. It doesn't matter. Even if I asked, she wouldn't tell me. She doesn't tell me anything.

"You almost cheated on me. You tried to cheat on me. How the actual fuck did this become about me?" She demands.

"Because the only reason I went to her is because of the secrets. I fucked up, even thinking about it. But this isn't all on me."

I lean forward, "This has to be more than good sex and superficial conversation, Peyton. As fucking awesome as that is, I can't just do that." I wait for her to say something—any fucking thing—to stop me. But she doesn't.

She sits there in silence and watches me as I walk out of the deli.

Chapter 12: After

Love--to me--
Is challenges and partners
And stories that make my heart skip
It's laughter and plans,
And dreaming.
(Rike's poems to Peyton)

I'm worried about what I'm wearing.

Which, all things considered, is the stupidest thing in the world to worry about. But it's ten and Rike will be here soon, and I want to look cute.

I'm in a wheelchair, and can't remember who the hell I am and I'm rocking a cast on my leg and arm, and I'm more concerned about what an idiot boy who wants in my pants will think than where I fucking come from.

"It's official, Collins. You're a fucking idiot," I mutter, brushing a lock out of my eyes.

I've put on makeup and my hair, though a bit scraggly, looks cute in its choppy piece around my face. For the first time in weeks, I feel vaguely human instead of like some desert island inhabitant.

It probably won't last long. I grab my notebook and the phone, and shove them into my purse, and a knock on the door has my heart jumping into my throat. I blink and it comes again. This time it's the kick I need to push myself forward and swing the door open for Rike.

He's got two cups of coffee, and his grin is lazy as it tracks over me. "Why did the chicken cross the basketball court?"

I tilt my head, a smile rising, "Why?"

"He heard the ref calling fowl."

I laugh, a surprised burst of noise, and he grins at me. "Good morning, sweetheart," he murmurs, and the nerves in my belly dip.

"You ready?" I ask, and his smirk deepens as he nods.

"Take these," he says, handing me the coffees and scooting around me. I catch the smell of him—crisp and soapy, with a hint of lead and smoke.

"Do you smoke?" I blurt as he pushes me out of the room.

He laughs softly, but doesn't answer my question until we're at the elevator and he can look at me. "No. I used to. But now it's mostly just the smell of it in my clothes from gigs."

I frown. "Gigs?"

He hesitates. "I'll show you, in the truck."

Curiosity mingles with nerves, and I nod, ducking and sniffing the coffee. It smell amazing and I make a tiny noise, almost a whimper.

"It's for you, Peyton. Although. Next time I hear that noise, I'd like to be balls deep inside you." I flush and Rike laughs. "God, that's new."

The little admission overrides my embarrassment, and my gaze snaps to his. "Is it?"

His gaze brightens, and he leans down as the door opens. Murmurs, "The first time I made you come, it was against my fingers on stage at Barrie's."

I bite my lip, trying very hard to stay still as that mental image works over me. "I find that highly unlikely," I say finally and he laughs at the unsteady note in my voice. Bastard.

"Sweetheart, you were always a dirty girl with an exhibitionist streak. It's one of the things I loved about you."

I flinch at that word. And he catches it. It seems like he catches everything.

Tommy is at the check-in counter, and he grins when he sees Rike pushing me through. "He gonna bring you home, Pey?"

I nod, and he waves amicably as we exit the hotel. There's a giant, hulking red truck, all shiny lines and clean leather interior, and Rike pushes me up to it. Eyes the truck and me. "I'm going to lift you in. Is that ok?"

When I'm settled and he's got my wheelchair in the back, he climbs in and reclaims his coffee. I'm quiet while he drives, watching him and taking in the truck.

It's clean, almost obsessively so. There is a notebook in the back, with two drum sticks and an open guitar case. I swivel to look at him, lifting my eyebrows.

He grins. "We play. Scott more than me—his record label hooked him up with a band, so he doesn't really *need* me the way he used to. But I still practice with him and do the occasional gig, especially for charity events. And I write all his songs, so I work closely with the band. It's how we met."

"I fell for a tattooed wannabe rock star?" I demand, disbelief thick in my tone. He laughs, a burst of surprise. Grins at me, and I shake my head. "You do realize that this is unlikely—I'm not that type of girl."

"I used to think that. It's why it took me three months to talk to you. Because I was pretty sure you weren't the type to fall for a tattooed boy with a shit past and a guitar. But you were always full of surprises. I think this one surprised you as much as it did me. Because that's exactly what you did. Fall for a bad boy with ink and a song."

I stare at him, and I shake my head. "No." His face tightens and I let out my breath. "I think you were always more than that. You're a songwriter. You're an artist. And the tattooed guitar might have caught my eye for a moment, but it would be who you are, not the pretty face you wear, that kept my interest."

He glances at me, and there's something new in his gaze. Wild hope that makes my chest tighten in a way that is almost painful. "That might be the most you thing you've said since you woke up, Fish."

That nickname again. I open my mouth to ask about it, but we're pulling up to the hospital, and he pulls us to a stop, sliding out of the truck almost before it fully stops. I see the grin on his lips when he does.

Slippery fucker likes his games.

***

Dr. Nedleman is fidgeting across from me. It's the first time we've met in the neurologist' office, and I come in on crutches, leg in a big black boot. It feels lighter than my cast, freeing, and still ungainly. I've knocked it on the wall three times already.

Rike sets my purse down next to me, and his blue eyes dart from the doctor to me and back again. Finally settle on me. "I'm gonna give you some time with Nedleman. Do you want to meet in Lindsay's room when you're done?"

I nod and flash a grateful, if tired, smile. He leans in, brushing a kiss over my hair, and then he's slipping out of the room. I focus on Dr. Nedleman and not the feel of Rike's lips and scratch of his beard.

"Are you having any breakthroughs, Peyton?" she asks hopefully.

"No. I know most of my past, up until I was about twenty. A few years are kinda hit or miss— some stuff I remember, and some I don't. And then it's all gone. The past three years. I don't remember. I know who my parents are and that I have siblings, but I'm not close to any of them. I know I've struggled with an eating disorder."

She shifts in her chair. "Yes. How are you doing with that?"

I shrug. "I haven't relapsed, if that's what you're asking."

"But you've reconnected with Rike."

I nod. "Not sure what that means. It would help if I knew who I was. And I've researched. Retrograde usually means that it's temporary. Memory should've come back by now. So why am I still a blank slate?"

She hesitates. "I don't know. It's just as baffling to me as it is to you." She spreads some documents across her desk. "I've studied your MRIs and the x-rays. There was no lasting damage done to your brain. No bruising or bleeds, no permanent loss."

"Except the memory," I say flatly.

She nods. "But what you need to remember is that the brain is a marvelous machine. And while yours is a bit faulty at the moment, there is nothing to say that this is permanent. The memories could be triggered by something as simple as smell or touch or a song. The more you're out there in the world, with the people who care about you, experiencing things and living, the more you'll remember. It might take years for it all to come back or it could come back tomorrow all at once. We can't say."

"And you can't help, right? I'm just stuck with this." She looks a little crestfallen, her smile wilting and her eyes dimming a little—almost like a puppy that's been scolded—and I wave a hand. "Don't look depressed, Doc. I'm not bitter. I'm just getting used to the new normal."

She nods, and gives me an uncertain smile. "This isn't forever, Peyton. And you are making progress. Being with Rike again—that will help."

I push to my feet, finding an unsteady balance on my crutches. "Thank you, Doc. I appreciate everything you've done to help me. If I ever come across someone with memory loss, I'll be sure to point her in your direction."

She laughs, and I leave the little office. I get around the corner, and lean against the wall. Concentrate, for just a few minutes, on nothing but breathing.

There isn't a magic cure. This is it. My new normal. I let out a shuddering breath and shove down all of the fear. Push off the wall, and crutch my way toward the room on the third floor where Lindsay is.

I don't get to dwell on how terrifying my normal is. Not when hers is so much worse.

The room is covered in flowers, and a trim blonde woman who looks like she could be Lindsay's older sister bustles by the door with another vase full of white roses, chattering a mile a minute. She sees me and her face goes as pale as the flowers she's carrying.

"Jim," she gasps, and a man lurches from the couch, snagging the flowers from her as she sweeps me into her arms, crying and laughing as she holds my head to her chest.

I don't know who the hell this woman is. I don't know why I matter to her. But I do know that being here, being held by her while she sobs and smiles at me like I'm the moon in the sky—it feels right. The same way Rike holding me feels right. But where I fight that feeling with him, with her I don't. I relax, my entire body wilting into hers as my arm comes around her and I cling to her. To the right that she represents.

"Ma. Let the poor girl breath. She doesn't remember me, and she's probably wondering why the hell she's being molested by a southern diva."

The woman laughs and steps back, dabbing at her eyes. She fixes a bright, watery smile on me and says, "I'm—"

"Jillian," I say and the whole room stills. I glance around and meet Rike's eyes, shocked and almost hurt where he's sitting in a chair near the window. Scott is leaning against it, and his hand lands on Rike's shoulder, holding him there as I swing my eyes back to Jillian and then to Lindsay. "Not Jillian?" I say lamely.

"You remember me?"

It clicks with a suddenness that makes me sway on my crutches, and Rike is moving, catching me before Scott can stop him. "Everyone give her a minute to breathe," he snaps, crouching in front of me. I'm perched on the edge of Lindsay's bed and his hands are tight on my knees as he kneels there. "What do you remember, baby?"

I can't look around. I can feel them watching me, the hopeful, hungry stares, and I don't want to admit the truth. I send Lindsay a pleading look.

"Rike, get out," Lindsay says abruptly. "Everyone. Out. I need a minute with my girl."

"Linds, not now," Rike growls.

"Yes, *now*. I let you play this your way and you fucked it all up. Now get out and let me talk to her." Rike doesn't move and she huffs. "Scotty."

It pulls the other guy off the window ledge, and toward the man kneeling at my feet. "Come on, man. Let her have this. It can't hurt, and you can get all your answers as soon as she's done. Come on. Jim. Jilly. Let's go." With a little effort and some cursing from Rike, he herds them out of the room, and it's just us.

She's quiet for a long minute. We both are.

"It figures you'd remember Ma. You've always adored her."

"I don't," I whisper. "I don't even know how I knew her name was Jillian. She just feels right—the way I feel around you. And it slipped out." I twist to look at her. "He's going to expect me to remember everything now, isn't he?"

"Yes," she says. "But he'll take what he gets. We all will. He wants you back, Pey. That's all any of us want."

I shift up on the bed, and land on her ankle. "Sorry," I say, lurching off, and she shrugs. Her face stays blank, except for the flare of sadness that slips over her for just a moment.

"How bad is it?" I ask.

"Bad."

"I've been a shitty friend, haven't I? I'm so sorry, Lindsay."

"Don't. It's my fault we're even here. I can't listen to you apologize on top of that. It is what it is— the hand we've got. We'll play it out, just like we always have."

I nod, and she tugs on my arm until I'm close enough that she can hug me, and I hold her. Neither of us mentions the tears that are spilled. Neither of us lets go, for a long time.

"Lindsay?"

"Hmm?"

"What were we doing that night?"

She releases me slowly. Meets my eyes, hers wide and cornflower blue. Assessing. "Are you sure you're ready to hear?"

"No. But I've been hiding in my little hotel room. It's comfortable and I don't really want to venture past it. It's safe, not knowing who the hell I am and how I ended up with Rike and you and Scott But. It' not really living, is it?"

She watches me for a moment. Then, "We were at my bachelorette party. A few girls I work with organized it; they were in the wedding. And you were trashed, because you were doing my shots. I wanted to be sober for the wedding."

"What happened?" I whisper.

She hesitates. And then she tells me everything.

Chapter 13: Before

I don't answer her phone calls. I'm too angry, and there's the simple truth. I want more than just a fun time. I think that's the worst part. That if she were any other girl, I wouldn't give a fuck. It wouldn't matter if Scott liked her or if I could share the important bits of my life with her. I wouldn't give a fuck that she was keeping so much from me. It would be almost a relief.

But because it's Peyton, and because she's been different from the very first time she stumbled into Barrie's, I care. I can't quit caring. And it's driving me batshit crazy.

So I ignore my phone and Scott ignores my moping and we both ignore the pointed stares Lindsay gives my phone when it rings. She's spending more time at our apartment. It makes me vaguely nervous. She's overlap in a relationship that I have very little control over.

There is a strange and unpleasant irony in the fact that I'm worried about Lindsay spilling secrets to a girl I'm angry at for keeping secrets.

I spend a week locked in my own head, pouring it all out into words I put to music. Because I've always been really fucking good at making music.

"Are you going to let me play these?" Scott asks on Monday night when I play through the riff on yet another 'you-broke-my-heart' anthem.

I shrug and he scrubs a hand through his hair. But he doesn't argue, just retreats with his guitar and listens while I strum on mine, making notes before I lose myself in a six-pack.

The tattoo shop is always quiet on Tuesday, which is why we prefer to head there then. A few guys are talking to Arsenal about a piece that they brought in, and I eye them warily. If I know anything about Arsenal, he'll flag me down in a few minutes.

Scott slides along the counter, careful not to touch it. Rabbit is a good dude, but he hates to have the display case coated in fingerprints.

"She's waiting," he grunts at us, and I nod briskly at him before following Scott towards the back stall.

"Rike. Can I get a minute?"

I slow and glance at Scott who nods subtly before I beak off to flank the tattoo artist. He holds up the sketch and I skim, trying to keep my face blank.

It's such a douchebag tat. A reaper with a scythe and a fucking crow. I glance at the guys. "Who is it for?"

"Me. I drew it up." The dark-haired dude is clean cut, and he flushes, rocking back on his heels nervously. Like he knows it's not good. "It's just an idea."

I stare at the drawing for a minute longer. "What does it mean?"

Twenty minutes later, I retreat as the guys make an appointment and Arsenal gives me a quick, muttered, "Thank you." I duck into the back stall where Scott is already laid out, his head pillowed on his arms while Staci goes to work.

"Did Arsenal need some artistic input?" she asks, and despite the fact that she's bent over my best friend's back, I can hear the gin in her tone.

"Yeah. Dude wants a reaper." She snorts and I nod. "I'm tweaking it. It'll be more Charon and the river Styx than reaper and birds, but he'll love it."

"Make sure Arsenal gives you a cut. That's original artwork so you know he'll charge for that shit."

I nod, but I don't plan on following through. I love the shop, and I love the art that goes into it. But I'm not so talented that I think I should be paid for my shit drawings. If some douchebag wants it tattooed on his back, that's his business, not mine.

"You good, bro?" I ask, and Scott grunts, a strained noise. I glance at what Staci is bent over and make a low noise of sympathy.

It hurts like a bitch to have your spine tattooed. I sit down in the corner of the booth, slumped on the ground, and listen to the rhythmic start and stop of the tattoo machine, the smell of ink and antiseptic filling my senses as all the stress of the week, of the fight with Peyton, slips away.

I fucking love this place. It's probably the only place I can get close to feeling what I do onstage, when there is only the high of the music and the energy of the crowd as they chant along to my songs.

"You know, you're a good artist," Staci says, her voice quiet as she works. "You'd do good here."

I blink out of my thoughts and stare at her. She's watching me with careful, bright eyes and I laugh, a startled noise. "You aren't serious."

"Why not? It'd be nice to work with a real artist, instead of someone who just copies the shit he finds online. You do good with the clients. And you're both here enough. Why the fuck not?"

I stare at her for a long moment, and then laugh. Shake my head.

"I think it's a good idea."

Her voice snaps my head up and Scott lifts his lazily, earning a swat from Staci while she barks, "Stay still, for fuck's sake."

I barely hear it. Peyton is standing in front of me, looking faintly sick to her stomach as she clutches her bag like a shield and stares at me with wide, wide eyes.

She's so fucking gorgeous it hurts, and seeing her, something in my gut settles, a shard that was out of place sliding where it belongs with a sick snick that makes my stomach churn and my head spin.

It feels right.

I told her I wanted to know now if this was just a distraction, wanted to know before it was too late to get out without getting hurt.

But staring at her, I know the truth. It's too late already. Maybe it's always been too late where she's concerned.

This girl will break me into a thousand pieces, and I won't even care. I'll shatter with a smile and thank her for the chance to care about her, even from a distance.

"What are you doing here?" I ask, pushing to my feet. She's standing close enough that when I rise, I'm almost pressed against her, and for a moment, all I can smell is sunshine and sugar and her. I sway close to her without meaning to.

"We need to talk," she says softly. I glance back at Scott. The session has just started and he'll be under Staci's machine for the next two hours, while she traces ink up and down his spine in intricate clockwork.

"Go," he says gritting his teeth when the needle bumps over his spine and I nod once. Grab her hand and pull her out of the stall and onto the sunlit sidewalk outside Dragon's Head Tattoo. I let her go almost immediately and she shifts, nerves playing over her features.

"Talk," I say and she lets out the breath she's been holding. I can hear the frustration in her huff, but I ignore it. I can't let myself care about that right now.

Even knowing I'm being an ass, I can't let myself care.

"You want to sit down or something?"

I shrug, and slip my shades on. It's a dick move, hiding behind the mirrored lenses. I do it anyway. "What are you doing here, Peyton?"

"I'm the daughter of a southern Baptist small town politician," she says, abruptly. "Daddy started out a doctor--had a real nice family practice. But it wasn't enough, and when I was in middle school, he went into politics. It became everything our family was. He was mayor and then our representative in the state legislature, and it just--it never ended. Every election was a new step and it didn't ever stop."

I stare at her, and she shrugs. "Everyone expected me to be a good little southern belle. Perfect Daddy's girl at the political dinners and events and rallies. And I was. I was really good at it. I played my perfect part really well."

There's something in her tone that has me nervous and I shift, reaching for her. She jerks back, out of my reach. "Just. Let me say this," she almost begs, and I nod.

"I hated it. I was good at it, and I did what they expected, but I hated it. I got involved in drugs. Nothing too serious, just shit that I knew would piss off my parents, if they were to find out. Binge drinking and random hookups." She laughs as my stomach churns. "Sometimes I think it's a miracle I made it through high school. I was the epitome of self-destructive. But the part that really fucked me and my parents up was the eating disorder." She takes a deep breath and digs into her bag, pulling out a beat up journal that she extends to me silently. "You want the truth. Want to know what I'm keeping to myself. It's in there."

I'm shaking my head and stepping away from her even while she's still speaking. Because I might want the truth, but I sure as fuck don't want it that way, because she thinks she has to give it to me. "I want it when you're ready to share," I growl.

"I'm never going to be ready to share this, Jokes. That's the thing. I hate who I was. It's why I left and came here. Why I don't talk about my past and where I came from, why I rarely go home, and have almost nothing to do with my family. Because I don't want to be that girl anymore and the only way I know how to be someone else is to *be* someone else. I don't keep you on the outside because I want you there. I keep you on the outside because I'm still trying to figure out who the hell I am."

"You're Peyton," I snap, fiercely, stepping into her and pulling her against my body with a hand on her waist. "You're mine and you're fucking perfect. I don't give a fuck what your past was."

She smiles sadly. "You do. You might not want to care, but you do. You can't help it. It pissed me off to no end that you almost fucked Lindsay. It was a fucked move. But I get it. I get why you were upset."

I stare at her and she lifts a hand, the tips of her fingers brushing over the stubble on my jaw, higher to push into my hair, and I lean into her, my forehead resting against hers. "It doesn't matter."

"Look at it. Read it. Then tell me that." She kisses me, a brief press of her lips and the hint of summer sweet sugar before she pulls back.

Chapter 14: After

It's carving my future into your
Skin, with lips and fingertips,
Twisting our lives together until there
Is no way to be
Anything but us.
Mapping the ink and curves
Of you until I know them
Like my own soul.
(Rike's poems to Peyton)

"You ok?" he asks, and I glance at him. I'm reeling from what Lindsay told me.

She was getting married. I was her best friend, the maid of honor, the only person in Austin she really cared about besides Scott and Rike. It was us four against the whole world and we were fucking winning.

It was us two, privileged debutantes, and them, bad boys with tattoos and a past that made me cringe. And we made it work. We thrived.

And then it shattered.

Sometimes, the fairy tale is too fucking good to be true.

That was the only time Lindsay sounded bitter. And she had been. She'd been furious. I get it, though. She was on the edge of having it all—and something as senseless as a distracted cab driver snatched it away.

I might recover. I might get my memories back. But Lindsay would never walk away from the devastation of the accident.

"How is Scott?" I ask. His gaze flicks to me, startled. I shrug. "What's happening to me doesn't affect just you, and his fiancée is in that hospital still. How is he dealing with everything?"

Rike blows out a breath and flicks the blinker on, hitting the highway and speeding up. "He's a mess," he says honestly. "He should be on his honeymoon, and riding the wave of his band's success. Instead, he's spent the last month figuring out how the hell to keep her from leaving him and how he's going to take care of her."

I jerk around, staring at him. "Why the hell would she leave him?"

"Because she's scared. Because she wants what's best for him and always has. She won't think that's her, now that she's in a wheelchair. Lindsay— she's the best thing that could have happened to Scott. But it's not easy being with him, and she won't be the person to make his life harder unnecessarily."

"But she loves him," I protest shrilly.

His gaze slides to me and a bitter smile tugs the corner of one lip up. "Sometimes love isn't enough, Peyton."

He hits the blinker again, swerving for the exit, and I clutch at the door of the truck. We're getting off the highway, and I glance out the window.

"Where are we? I thought we were going to get lunch."

"We are," he say.

The house he pulls up to is in a well-cared for neighborhood. The grass is a dirty green, and the flowerbeds a little overgrown, but there's a wraparound porch with comfortable looking patio furniture, and a privacy fence hides the backyard.

I look at Rike, confused, and he grins at me. "I didn't say where we were going, sweetheart. But this has been your favorite place to have lunch since the day we moved in."

"This is our home?" I whisper, even though I know. Of course it is. What else could it possibly be?

There is a tiny part of me, staring at this gorgeous house, that wants to race inside and soak it all in. Remember everything. Lie in the bed where I was happy.

A bigger part—the larger part—is terrified, and for a moment, I'm stuck to my seat, staring.

Rike pulls open the door and holds out his hand. His eyes are hopeful. And before I consciously make the decision, I put my hand in his and let him pull me from the truck. Against his body, all hard and hot against my own.

"Are you going to behave if we go in there?" I ask huskily, and then flush. I can't believe I just asked that.

A slow smile curls his lips. "Do you want me to?"

I laugh, and step back. Because I'm a little terrified about how much I really don't want him to.

"Come on," he says, handing me the crutches and pacing me up to the door. I kinda love the way he's so carefully attentive, his hand on the small of my back to brace me as I make my way up the three stairs to the front door before he swings it open.

The house is messy—not terribly surprising considering that I've been in the hospital. And it's huge. I glance at Rike. "Did we live here alone?"

"No. It was originally a house with an apartment, and we thought it'd be perfect for us. The apartment has a small kitchen, so when we want privacy, we just go upstairs. And your studio is in the garage loft. Scott and I keep most of our shit in the garage, and that's where he'll practice with the band when they're just fucking around. Lindsay works downtown, so she didn't get an office, but we all have our space. And when we don't want the space, we're together."

His eyes are bright and almost stupid happy as he talks about it and I can see it, can picture the life he's painting out.

"Where is our room?" I ask, softly.

His eyebrows go up, and he points toward the back of the house.

"Do you want to see it?" The question is soft and very vulnerable.

"No," I say. "Not today." He nods and steps into the large kitchen. Pulls a bowl of soup from the fridge and starts heating it, and pouring us both tea. He's efficient and brisk in his movements, a graceful poetry in motion doing something so simple and mundane.

But there is nothing simple or mundane about Rike. He's gorgeous, with his shaggy black hair and the beard that is growing on me. The tattoos curving on his long, strong arms and licking across the skin over his fingers.

He's everything I never expected to want, but this feels familiar. He's who I chose. This unconventional, beautifully confusing life.

Scott and Lindsay.

They are the life I chose.

"How did we get here?" I whisper, and Rike's gaze snags mine. I shake my head, helplessly. "This isn't what I pictured, Rike. This is nothing like I imagined my life. And I understand that it's what I chose. But I don't remember, and I can't reconcile it." His expression falls, and I make a tiny noise, reaching for him. "I am trying, Rike. I just—it's a lot."

"I know," he whispers. "I want to help, but I don't know how. I don't know how to give you the space you need when all I want is to bring you home."

I reach for him and catch his hand, twisting our fingers together. He stares at our fingers, until the microwave dings and it jerks both of us out of our thoughts.

The soup and crusty bread he brings out is delicious, creamy potato broth with a spicy sausage. But the tension between us strings tight and uncomfortable, and it makes my stomach twist, until I finally put the food down.

Rike is waiting, because as soon as I stop eating, he shifts, gathering the bowls and taking them to the sink.

"There's some stuff in your office. I think you should look at it. Will you come upstairs with me?"

I nod, and he grins, shifting over to me and lifting me up from the chair.

"What are you doing?" I breathe out as he cradles me against his chest.

His eyes are so close, so blue I could get lost in them, and I have to look down, because I can't get lost. Not yet. Not until I've found myself.

"Stairs, sweetheart. I'll carry you up."

The loft is captivating. Half-finished canvases sit on easels, a sketch and tiny cut piece of papers waiting to be assembled cover a large table, and sculptures clutter a corner in various states of finish. A stained glass window filters light in, beautiful and ethereal, and I feel like I'm in a church. Like this is where I am supposed to worship, and where everything is right. Rike sets me on a deep red leather chaise lounge in a corner of bookshelves and I shiver. The table next to the chaise holds a notebook.

He follows my gaze. "You wrote constantly. Sometimes it was things you'd share with me or Linds, but it was usually just for yourself, and it was incessant."

"Do you think that reading the journals could help me remember?" I ask.

He nods without hesitation. "Yes. And they're yours. Please. Go through them."

I nod and shift back, getting comfortable against the chair, and he smiles, his eyes soft. "I remember when I bought that chair for you. It was right after we moved here, and we had been out, downtown. You saw it at this tiny place that sold art and you fixated. Brought it up every few days for weeks. So I went down and picked it up one night after I finished a pretty big piece on a client. Surprised you with it. It was like watching a kid on Christmas morning. I fell in love with you a little more that day." He laughs, a little, at himself. "I fell in love with you a little more every day, Peyton."

I make a tiny noise, and his gaze snaps to me.

Later, when I think about it, I'll be sure he moved first. But the truth is we moved at the same time. I reach for him at the same time he wraps a hand around my neck, lifting me up.

His lips meet mine, and the world explodes. Everything is about him, about the rough urgency of his lips against mine, and his hands that shift me, just the right angle to my head. His tongue licks over the seam of my lips and I gasp, and he's everywhere, his tongue tangling with mine.

He's not just kissing me. He's devouring and conquering, claiming me. And I make a tiny little noise, almost a mewl, and let him.

His body comes down, knees on either side of me, and I want more of his weight, more of that maddening lazy tongue, more of his clever fingers, brushing over my skin, everywhere and nowhere.

"More," I gasp, and he grins against my lips.

"More what, perfect girl?" he murmurs. "Tell me what you want."

Tell him what I want? How the hell am I supposed to do that? I shake my head and his lips skate down my jaw, over my throat in wet, nipping kisses that have me aching. He pushes my shirt, a blue button-down over a white, lace-trimmed cami, aside, and his fingers are on my breasts, circling and circling, endless torture. "Do you want my mouth here?" he murmurs, and I flush.

Why can't he just fuck me? Why must he hear it? His fingers ghost over my nipple, pinch sharply, and I gasp, "*Yes.*"

Rike makes a low growl and yanks my cami down, shoving aside the pale pink bra cup and I moan as the wet heat of his mouth closes over me, pulling hard on my nipple. His teeth rake over it and I almost come off the damn chaise. His hands are moving, one cupping my breast through the clothes, the other skating lower, sliding under the hem of my shirt to play over my torso. His tongue circles my nipple, slow and lazy, and I jerk on his hair, pulling him up and kissing him. He groans, and I can almost feel him fighting to pull away. His gaze is clouded and hungry when he demands, "What do you want, Peyton? Do you want my fingers"—he brushes against me over my jeans with his fingers and I shiver—"or do you want my tongue?" I shudder, my head falling back. A low chuckle rolls over me. "Tell me, sweetheart. Tell me what you want. Tell me how bad you want to come riding my lips."

I shake my head and he unzips my jeans, and slips a hand inside. I scream as his fingers slip through me, playing over me, and his thumb rubs over my clit.

"Say it, Peyton," he demands hoarsely. "Say what you want."

"You," I whimper.

He curses. "Not enough. Tell me you want me to tongue fuck you. That you want to taste yourself on my lips when I'm inside you. Tell me."

His fingers move again and I growl, "Fucking do it or don't. Get me off or don't but don't fucking toy with me. Yes, goddammit, I want you to eat me out until I come."

He grins, and moves, faster than I can really process. One second he's hovering above me, and the next he's between my thighs, my jeans hanging around my ankles as he lowers his head and then nothing matters. There is only the glide of his tongue against me, the fluttering pressure as he tongues my clit, and the slow thrust of his fingers. He licks at me, the tip of his tongue circling, until I have my hands in his hair and my body is moving, writhing against him as he uses lips and tongue and teeth to drive me fucking insane.

My whole body is tight, and I gasp when he thrusts into me with his tongue, my vagina clenching down when he pinches my clit, a delicious agony.

His fingers are against my ass, smoothing over my cheeks as his tongue fucks into me, and he slaps me, a sharp hard slap, and I splinter, screaming as I come, a wave of sensation that rips through me. He's rising before my heartbeat slows, and he kisses me.

And despite the tiny voice screaming at me to stop, I lick at his lips, at the taste of me on his tongue.

He slams into me while we're kissing, and my body goes tight, arching off the chaise against the delicious pressure, the exquisite fullness of him inside me. He groans, and drops his head down against mine. I fucking love the feel of his beard bristling against my breast as he struggles to catch his breath.

"You're fucking tight, baby," he whispers.

I shift, my hips moving in a tiny circle and he groans. "Don't," he begs. "Go slow."

"Fuck slow," I snap. "Fuck me."

It breaks whatever control he has left—his hand catches in my hair and he pulls my head back, kissing me hard, a bruising kiss that has my head spinning as his big body thrusts into me.

He knows my body. Knows just how to fuck me. Each thrust ends on a tight twist of his hips, hitting a spot deep inside that I didn't realize I had, until I'm panting, begging as he fucks me. "Rike," I groan, and I reach for him, all the achy need in me bubbling up.

I bite him. Hard. And he grunts, a deep hungry noise. Shoves me down and fucks me hard, until I'm tossed into orgasm, my body writhing against his mindlessly.

"Yeah," he groans, "just like that. Fuck me just like that, baby."

I'm clinging to him, my nails in his shoulders as I meet his thrusts, the orgasm spinning on and out and then he groans, a long noise, goes still and tight above me. His face drops, so I can see him through the shaggy hair and the beard and—

He's fucking beautiful. Gentle, and so fucking vulnerable, as he comes inside me with a low groan that I can feel in my toes. Staring at me while he comes.

When it's over, he falls to the bed next to me, and gathers me into him, sighing. A content noise.

I lay awake for a long time after he's asleep, wondering just how badly I've fucked things up now.

Chapter 15: Before

Here's what I learn, reading the journal she left with me:

Who she was doesn't matter.

Facing the truth is fucking painful.

She is the bravest girl I've ever met.

It takes me three days to get through the journal because it's hard as fuck to read. There are a few times, reading it and looking at the pictures, that I have to bolt for the toilet before I throw up.

How did she go from *this* shell of a girl, this walking corpse, to the girl who is so vibrant and alive, whose passion and daring make my head spin? I am trying to wrap my head around something that makes no fucking sense.

I realize, with almost sickening quickness, that I loathe her family.

Seeing her past on paper, seeing the demons she fought and how much she hated who she was being molded into--I've never met them, and part of me hopes I never do. I don't know how to be in the same room as someone who had the chance to care for a girl like Peyton and who fucked it up so completely.

"I want to sing tonight," I say, staring blankly at the photo clipped to the inside of the journal.

Scott glances at me, at the picture, before he nods. "Do what you think is best, man."

I offer him a sick smile and shove to my feet.

"She trusted you," he says before I leave the room. "Are you going to return the favor?"

I look at him. I know what he's asking. "It's not only my story to share," I say carefully.

"Don't hide behind that," he says. "Do what you think needs to be done. I want you to be happy,

Rike. Whatever that means. And this girl—she makes you happy. In a way I haven't seen since we were eight."

When we were eight we had been living in a group home, and he'd been the shit head who picked a fight. We beat each other senseless, but when it was time to take the fall, neither of us was willing to throw the other under the bus. It was the first time in my life someone had my back and I never forgot it.

We were separated a year later, tossed into separate foster homes that got progressively worse. But for that six months, we had each other. We weren't so fucking alone.

We were miserable little shits the world didn't want, but we were fucking happy.

I let out the breath I've been holding and nod at him. "Thanks, Scott."

***

The crowd is high on the music. Scott played through our first set, setting the tone and getting them riled up with anthem after anthem, an ode to the summer that is fading away. Lindsay is swaying in the corner booth, next to a pale Peyton in a tiny dress that's driving me to distraction. She's got a drink in front of her, but she hasn't touched it.

Scott flicks a look at me when the song ends and his eyebrow lifts in question. I nod, and hit the cymbals. The girls on the dance floor sway and scream, and he laughs, a low, husky noise that will have them squirming in their skirts.

Fucking player. If he's not careful, Lindsay will rip his balls off and feed them to him.

I laugh at that thought.

"We've got a treat for you tonight. My boy Rike has been working on a new song. Most of the time, he lets me do the singing, but I think it's time to remind you all that the boy has mad skills that don't involve the sticks. So. Give it up, ladies. Rike it's all you, brother."

I come out from behind the drum set and Scott wraps me in a quick, rough hug. "Kick ass, bro," he mutters before dropping off the stage.

I let out a breath, and sink onto the stool. Adjust the mic. I can feel the entire room, all of them waiting for me to say something. Anything. But I can't see past the glare of the house lights.

It doesn't matter. I don't need to see to know where she is and that she's watching me with big, sky blue eyes. I close my eyes, picturing her.

And I sing.

I've always been good at creating and shit at saying what I feel. Maybe because of how I was raised. But tonight, I'm trying my best to let go of that.

Perfect girl,

She sits and listens,

And I can't help but see everything that she's hiding.

She's beautiful and broken,

Tears she tries to hide,

And I can't help but wonder what's on the inside

You're broken and lovely,

Fire and ice,

And holding you is painful,

But the payoff is worth the price,

Because you're everything to me,

Yes, you're everything to me,

Perfect girl.

Everyone said she was wrong,

When she danced to a song only she heard,

And I just want to sing along to the music of her soul,

Because she's beautiful and broken, with the tears she tries to hide.

You're broken and lovely,

Fire and ice,

And holding you is painful,

But the payoff is worth the price,

Because you're everything to me,

Yes, you're everything to me,

Perfect girl.

And all of us are broken, all of us are flawed,

All of us have battles, and times when we fall.

And I will love you always, with scars and broken heart,

You're beautiful and broken, my perfect girl.

You're broken and lovely,

Fire and ice,

And holding you is painful,

But the payoff is worth the price,

Because you're everything to me,

Yes, you're everything to me,

Perfect girl.

I strum the final notes of the song and as the music dies, I'm aware, painfully aware, of the quiet that surrounds me, a heavy blanket over the bar. I blink, opening my eyes and staring out into the room, to where I know she is.

The room comes alive like a fucking wave, a roar of noise that crests over me and drowns out Scott as he bounds onto the stage and shoves my hand up, yelling my name for the half-drunk fans who already know it.

I give a mocking half-bow because it's expected, and he shoves be back to my drum kit, his eyes alive with excitement. I sit, dizzy suddenly. Exhausted.

I poured fucking everything into that song.

When I glance at the booth, my heart drops, the high of the song, and the crowd, and even Scotty, fading away. It's like a punch to the gut.

She's not there.

Chapter 16: After

It's long nights next to you

And hearing your sighs

The sweetest music,

My favorite song the sound of your

Name whispered from the darkness.

The taste of wine and you,

and quiet noise of my pleading.

It is wild and reckless and soft

And sweet and

Always,

You.

(Rike's poems to Peyton)

The journals are a revelation. I spend the next several days poring over them, hiding in my hotel room. Trying to forget everything that happened in the loft. Rike gives me time and space, which I appreciate. Reading the journals is like getting to know myself.

I can watch myself falling in love, living through fights. Forming a bond with a girl I would never have chosen as my best friend.

And that's the thing. Rike isn't who I would have chosen. Neither is Lindsay. I don't understand where Scott fits in our weird little world but I know that he is important to Rike and therefore to me.

I always thought that I would have a quiet, traditional life, one like my parents had, even if they were miserable. I expected that, maybe because it's what was expected of me. But this—this isn't quiet. This isn't traditional.

I'm a fucking artist, a girl who spends her days painting and sculpting and taking photos. Writing. And maybe I didn't need to because my boyfriend was doing such a good job of taking care of us, but I was good at it.

And I loved it. All of it.

If there's anything I learn from the journals, it's that I loved the weird little life we built.

The phone next to me buzzes to life, Rike's face brightening the screen. I stare at it for a minute, contemplating answering, before it goes silent and takes the option away. I can't think of him without remembering everything he made me feel. The way his hands played across my body, pulling pleasure from it so fucking effortlessly.

The problem isn't that I don't want Rike, and everything that comes with him. Wild, beautiful chaos.

The problem is it's all I want. I lie awake at night, crying because I know that we were happy. And I can't remember it. I feel like I've been robbed, and like every moment I spend in that life is a lie—me pretending something that I want but don't feel. Not really.

He would probably tell me I'm thinking too hard. To let go of my worry and just live. But I don't know how. And it's terrifying.

The phone rings again, and I frown. The number isn't one I know.

"Hello?"

"Holy shit, I finally found you. Jesus, baby girl, you shouldn't make it so fucking hard to get a hold of you. Where are you?"

I blink once. Twice. Finally, "Um. Who is this?"

There's a loud laugh and then, "Oh shit. That's right. Ok. It's Brody, Peyton. I'm in town. Where are you?"

Chapter 17: Before

It takes a long time for us to break away—longer than normal. Everyone is high on the fucking song.

Scott doesn't say anything about it until we're finally free. His gaze rakes over me. "You surprised me back there, RIke."

"You've heard me work," I say, and he laughs.

"Not on that. That was shit you haven't bothered to share with me."

I shrug. "It came to me this morning."

"They loved it."

"Doesn't matter, does it? The girl it's for didn't even hear it."

He eyes me briefly and then shakes his head. Falls to silence as we walk through the dark streets back to the apartment. Something is going on with him, but I don't know what and I'm too fucking tired to puzzle it out.

I poured my soul into that song. And to realize she wasn't even there to hear it…I lash out suddenly, hurling the glass beer bottle I'm holding. It swings in a shining arc before it shatters against the side of a barber shop, glass and beer spraying out. Scott side-eyes me but doesn't comment, and with the explosion of glass, some of my temper settles.

"Come on, dude," he says, pulling me along.

"Why didn't she listen?" I ask, and it occurs to me that I'm too drunk for maudlin shit. Or maybe that's why I'm descending into maudlin shit. Either way. It's a bad recipe give the way the night is shaking out.

"I dunno, man. But don't jump to shitty conclusions. You both keep doing that and you're going to fall apart because of them. Talk to her tomorrow. Find out why."

"You're such a fucking girl," I laugh and he shrugs. Accepting it.

We're emotionally stunted shits, but Scott isn't stupid. He's been through the court-ordered psych shit. He knows that communicating is the only way for either of us to build something healthy and longer than a few nights.

He just hasn't ever cared.

I watch him while he unlocks the door to our walkup.

My badass best friend who doesn't care about anything but strumming his guitar and picking up pussy is growing up. What the actual fuck.

He grins at me, a quick glimpse of the dude who always had my back, and the thought slips away as he pushes open the door.

Lindsay is sitting on the couch, her legs crossed under her. She isn't wearing a bra, which is vaguely distracting.

I've seen the girl naked, and I can see her nipple through the tank top she's wearing.

Then Peyton steps out of the kitchen, carrying a red plastic cup and wearing a nervous expression and bare feet.

Her eyes find mine as my mouth falls open, and I hear Linds giggle, a triumphant noise that is vaguely grating as I cross the tiny living room in two steps and yank Peyton into my arms.

Her hands are in my hair before my lips hit hers, pulling me into the kiss, and the world falls away.

She's pressed against me, all soft curves and rumpled skirt and sharp nails digging into my scalp. She tastes so fucking sweet—sugar and sunshine as her tongue tangles with mine, fighting to control the kiss. Her nails sink down, yanking on my hair and I bite her lower lip, just enough to make her moan and sag against me.

I drink down that noise like fucking water. I want to hear every sound she makes, and what causes them, want to know how demanding she will be when I've got her riding the edge of orgasm, when my tongue is driving her fucking crazy.

She sways against me, her hips grinding against my erection as she all but purrs into the kiss. I pull back, just enough to stare at her, at the hot hunger in her eyes. "You heard it."

She nods, and tears well in her eyes. I make a low noise in the back of my throat, and kiss her again. Softer. Gentle.

"Meant every fucking word, perfect girl," I whisper. I can feel her tears on my cheeks, rolling down between us, can taste them as I kiss her.

I shift my grip and lift her by the ass and her legs wrap around me, clinging to me as I kiss her.

Vaguely, I'm aware of Lindsay, her voice rising in question and Scotty pulling her away. But it's all very distant, overshadowed by the girl in my arms and her lips moving over mine in a hungry, desperate way that makes my blood heat.

I walk without looking, until the darkness surrounds us and my knees hit the edge of my bed. Without breaking the kiss, I kick the door shut behind me and then lower her to the bed.

I pull back, just enough to stare at her. I've waited too long for her to not savor the sight.

Peyton in my bed, her hair spread over the pillow, her eyes foggy as she reaches for me, is the most erotic thing I've ever seen.

"Rike," she whispers, and I groan, dropping down on her and kissing her. My lips eat her up, my tongue pushing past her lips, tangling with hers as I rock against her. She's all soft curves and sweet smooth skin against my dick, and I want to pull back until she says my name again in that pleading tone that I can't get enough of, but I can't pull myself away from her.

She's fucking addictive and I want to lick every inch of her. My hand comes up, yanking on the neckline of her tank, pulling it and her bra down until her breast spills out, filling my hand, and I growl as she arches against me, rubbing like a kitten. Her nipple is a tight little peak against my palm and I leave her lips as I trail wet kisses down her.

She gasps when I draw her nipple into my mouth, scraping my teeth over the sensitive skin before I suckle her. I slid a hand between us, and her hips tilt up into my touch as I slip my hand under her shorts and into her panties.

"Fuck, you're wet, babe."

"I want you," she whimpers, and I laugh, a low noise as I shove my fingers into her and she shrieks, choking it off with a hand over her lips.

I pull it free. "Baby girl, I want to hear every fucking noise you make when I fuck you."

I slip my fingers through her, teasing, almost out, and she gasps, "But, Sc—"

I smirk, and whisper against her ear, "Will fucking hear everything. And like it."

She shudders, her pussy clenching around my fingers, and I lick the shell of her ear as I rub her clit and fuck her with two fingers. "You fucking love that, don't you, sweetheart? Knowing he's listening to me fuck you. She is, too."

"Rike," she whimpers, and I bite her earlobe, and she shrieks, her body arching off the bed as she scrambles against me, thrusting against my hand, and I laugh, watching her come apart.

I pull my hand free before while she's catching her breath, my hand sticky and wet. I almost lick my fingers clean. Instead I yank her shorts down, and sink to my knees by the bed, pulling her to my lips.

She screams when I cover her with my lips, and I laugh as she surges against me.

Very far away, I can hear my friend cursing, and then everything fades away until there is only her, and me, and this bed. Her hands in my hair and her voice, cursing and panting and begging as she moves against me. Her ankles on my shoulders, digging in as I lick her. Nip at her and suck on her clit, until she's screaming again, her body moving in waves across the bed, and all I can smell is sugar and sunshine.

She comes like no one else, an orgasm so fucking gorgeous I could spend all day and night getting her off just to watch her fall apart. She's panting, a sexy sheen of sweat covering her. I smile, place a kiss against her thigh and crawl up her body.

"You're so fucking gorgeous," I whisper and she smiles, a drowsy, sweet thing as she pulls me to her lips. She licks across my lips, kissing me deeply, her tongue twisting into my mouth as her hips roll in tight little waves against me. The little purr of satisfaction she gives makes me groan, my dick twitching against her, and she laughs, reaching down to tug at my jeans. "Off," she demands, and I scramble to obey.

She props herself up as I strip and I hesitate as her eyes go wide and hungry when I'm naked. She licks her lips and sits up, reaching for me. "I want you in my mouth," she whispers.

My dick jerks, and I shove her back on the bed, rolling a condom on before I settle over her as she shifts restlessly. "Next time," I say and push into her.

She screams and I laugh, a noise that sounds erotic and choked even to my ears. She's tight and hot, so fucking wet it's easy as hell to slip into her silky heat, and my dick has never felt so fucking good.

Sex has never felt so good.

"Fuck, you're perfect," I pant, and she whimpers. "How do you want it, sweetheart? You want slow and easy?" I slide out and she groans, whining as I slip back, so deep and slow it's almost torture.

"Fuck me, Rike," she hisses, her nails scrambling along my back.

She's marking me and it's hot as fuck. I shove into her, and she screams.

God, she puts on a good fucking show for them to listen to. It's hot as fuck, knowing Scott is listening as I fuck this girl. I grin and let go, flying on the feel of her wrapped around me, the sting of her nails and teeth in my shoulder, the scent of her as she rolls her hips against me. It's not going to last long— I've waited too long for this and I'm so fucking ready for her. I shift her, so I'm on my knees, her legs wrapped around me as I thrust into her, and slip a hand between us, rubbing her clit as I pinch her nipple.

She screams again, her pussy clamping down on my dick, and I growl, thrusting into her hard as my orgasm tackles me. All I can hear is her and the sound we make together, the scent of sex all around us, and it's so fucking good I never want anyone else.

I fall onto her, and she puffs out a sigh, giggling as I crush her into the bed. I kiss her and roll to the side, pulling her with me so I don't slip out of her. She makes a tiny noise of pleasure and arches against me a little.

For a long minute, all we do is stare at each other, and breathe.

She's here. She heard my song.

She's fucking *here*, in my arms.

"You think so loudly," she murmurs, reaching up and running her thumb over my jaw. I turn my head just a little, nuzzling into her palm, and her eyes go soft and distant.

"What am I thinking?" She hesitates, and shakes her head. Retreating without ever moving. I run my fingers through her hair, and whisper, "I'm thinking that it's amazing. That having you here is fucking amazing. Everything I've wanted and refused to allow myself to believe would happen."

"I've offered," she says, her tone dry.

I catch her face in my hand, studying it. The tiny nose, slightly upturned and dusted with freckles, the big eyes that are just now a little bit afraid.

"I'm not good for you, Fish," I say.

She blinks, startled. "Did you just call me a fish?"

I nod and roll us. "It's a quote I heard once. 'People say there are other fish in the sea. I say, fuck you, she was my sea.'" I shrug. "It stuck with me."

She propped herself up on my chest and gives me a frown. "Wouldn't that make me the sea? Not a fish."

I slap her ass lightly and she yelps, her eyes flying wide. "Shut up. Fish sounds better."

She wiggles and, deep inside her, my cock twitches. I'm half-hard again, hungry for more of her, and as her gaze goes lazy, I know she's with me.

She rocks slowly, and I grip her hips lightly, letting her set the pace as she works me. "What does all this mean?" she whispers.

"What do you want it to mean?"

Doubt flickers in her eyes for a heartbeat, and I pinch her nipple, jerking her gaze back to me and the moment. "What do you want?" I demand.

"I want you to fuck me. I want us to have fun and hang out and see what happens." She hesitates. "I want to be that girl you sang about, Rike. But I don't know if I can be."

I shrug and pull her down to my lips, "You already are, Fish. But we can do easy right now. I'm not going anywhere."

Gratitude flares in her eyes before I kiss her, a deep kiss that says everything she isn't ready for—all the things I said in a song. That she's everything. I would fucking hang the moon for this girl.

When I finally break the kiss, she's panting, and her hips are moving in small, restless circles. I smirk at her. "Wanna give them another show?"

"You're a kinky bastard, aren't you?"

She grins and I nod. Groan when she rises on my dick, until only the head is inside her, and she's panting, these broken little noises as she just lingers there. My hands are on her again, cupping her breasts, and I lick over a nipple.

She screams, her whole body shuddering as she slides down my cock, hard, and my teeth close on her nipple, and I laugh as she fucks me.

I might be a kinky bastard, but she fucking loves it.

Chapter 18: After

The problem is that I am
Never content.
I want more than your smiles
and sweet words, more than your mind
I want to be your first and last thought,
the laughter in your eyes, and safe
haven you long for.
the press of lips you remember upon waking.
(Rike's poems to Peyton)

Brody has grown up.

That's the thing that hits me the hardest. My brother has grown up.

When he steps into the hotel room, he ignores it completely, his gaze narrowed on me.

In theory, I know what Brody should look like: a gangly, teenager with a sly smirk and laughing eyes.

That's the brother I remember, the one who kept me sane through the hell that was high school and growing up as the daughter to a political family.

The man who stands in front of me. He's taller than me, long and lean, with a buzz cut hairstyle that screams military, and a sharp gaze that misses nothing as it takes me in.

A smirk turns his lips and I let out a tiny sob. Because just like that, there he is. My baby brother. He opens his arms, and I crutch across the room to hug him. "God, I missed you," I mutter. "Where the hell have you been?"

"Working," he says noncommittally, and pulls back. "Why the hell are you in this shithole? I tried the house first, but it looks deserted."

"Scott hasn't been there much. I don't know where Rike is," I say.

His eyebrows go up and he frowns. "How the hell do you not know where Rike is? Why isn't he here?"

Because I'm terrified, because I don't know how to be with him, because I want him so much it's scary. I don't say any of that. Just chew on the inside of my cheek while Brody stares at me, and I can watch him puzzle through it, putting the pieces where they belong.

He sighs. "How much did you forget, Pey?"

"Everything. Everything from that last stint in rehab to when I woke up. I remembered Lindsay's mom's name, but I couldn't tell you why. I remember that I don't like Mom and Dad."

He snorts. "You'd have to be dead to forget that sweetheart. I assume that's why you didn't call them?"

I nod and he grins.

"Good call. So. Tell me what you want."

I shake my head. "I don't know." I've thought, so often, about calling Brody. But he's always been the one to push me, to demand my very best even when he love me at my worst. It's why I haven't called. I can't be my best right now.

"Do you want to go home? Or do you want me to get you away from everything for a while so you can get a grip on things?"

He's watching me, closely enough that he sees the hope flare in my gaze, and he smirks. "Ok. Then let's pack you up and get out of here. Ok?"

And just like that, a chapter of my life is closed. Brody goes to work packing up the books and clothes and shit I have in the hotel room, and I direct as much as I can while he ignores me. Tommy comes by and I cry a little, saying goodbye to him. I know that it isn't the last time I'll see him, that I have his phone number to call him. That eventually, my life will settle.

But for now, I'm running and there's no room for him.

And because he's always been amazing, and just what I need, he merely smiles and waves at me as I drive away with Brody.

My brother eyes me as we hit the expressway that will take us away from Austin.

Away from Rike.

"Are you sure this is a good idea?" I nod, and he lets out a deep sigh. "Ok. But there's no harm in being wrong. You can change your mind. And when you do, I'll still love you. I'll bring you home, without a word. Do you understand?"

I twist my head to look at him. I do. My brother is an absolute gem. "How did I get so lucky to have a brother like you?" I ask softly.

He laughs. "Well, God had to give you something to compensate for the rest of the family."

Chapter 19: Before

"But what the hell is wrong with the couch we have?"

I swallow my laugh as Scott glares across the apartment full of boxes and empty beer cans.

Lindsay narrows her eyes and stares at her boyfriend. "I was one of your one-nighters, Scotty. I'm not a fucking idiot, and that piece of shit pussy magnet is not going to be in my house!"

"I like my couch!"

She pops a hip out and crosses her arms, eyebrows climbing as Peyton comes out of the kitchen with two beers. She's laughing. "Do you like getting your dick sucked? Because if you keep that? We're out. I've still got my room at the sorority house."

"Couch goes, bro," I say from the floor where I'm assembling Peyton's bookshelves.

"You are so fucking whipped, man," Scott says.

I shrug, and Peyton sashays over to me, leaning down to kiss me briefly. "He's not whipped."

"No, baby. I'm whipped. And if he got to fuck you, he'd be whipped too."

She flushes and I laugh. Even after six months together, she's still slightly scandalized by the laissez-faire approach Scott and I have to sex.

When her clothes are on. When I've got her naked in my bed, all of that good, proper girl melts away.

"Do we at least get to help pick the damn thing?" Scott demands and Lindsay smirks. I swallow my laugh as I stand, pulling a finished bookcase with me.

"You already picked it, didn't you?" I say, and she flashes me a wide smile.

"It'll be delivered in the morning, so y'all need to finish this room before then."

Scott curses and I let out a heavy sigh. "Linds, that's just dirty. At least give us a little time."

She shrugs and turns back to the kitchen. "I've got another four boxes in here. Have fun, boys."

I shake my head and look at Scott. "You really need to control that girl."

"Fuck you, dude," he snaps. "Get that box out of my way."

I move the box of clothes. Scott is pissy, which is making the whole process of moving even more hellish than normal.

But he's directing all that anger at Lindsay. It would bother me more, except I know what she's doing. I've been watching her single-handedly manipulate my boy for half a year, and if there is anything I'm sure of, it's that Lindsay Illian knows exactly what she's doing when she pushes Scott around.

Giving him something to be pissy about keeps him focused on her and not on the terrifying elephant in the room.

We're moving in together.

It was her idea, although I know Peyton had a hand in it. And it makes sense. The new school year is starting, and they spend more time at our place than anywhere else. I knew all the reasons why it was a good idea, all the reasons on paper. Saving time and money, and practicality.

It was still terrifying, and part of me wanted to bolt. As much as I adored Peyton, as sure of her as I was, I had never lived with a woman. I'd lived in group homes, and by myself, and with Scott. I had never wanted to live with anyone else.

"Where does this go?" Scott asks, holding a big box with Peyton's handwriting on the side.

"Our room," she says bouncing on her toes. She cuts her eyes at me. "I got new sheets for our bed."

And that. That right there settles me. Because no matter what else there is, I'm doing this with her. A girl who I've got no fucking doubts about. And the idea of her in my bed, in my space, all the time—it's more intoxicating than it is infuriating.

I slap a screwdriver against Scott's chest and grin. "Come on. We need to get the table put together before that couch arrives."

He looks vaguely sick, but he follows me.

***

My whole body hurts when we finally quit for the day. It took two days and enough coffee to give me an ulcer, but we're done. Everything is out of our old place, and aside from the couple boxes of random shit no one knows what to do with, the new place is set up. Linds even cooked a first meal for us.

And Peyton has kept me out of our room as she worked on it for most of the evening, shouting for

Lindsay and even Scott when she needed help and shoving me away every time I tried to sneak a peek. She's almost vibrating with excitement now as she shifts from foot to foot in front of the closed door, her wide blue eyes searching mine and nervous.

"Babe, you don't need to be nervous," I say, pulling her into me. "All I need is you and a warm bed."

She shakes her head, her brow furrowed. It's this adorable look she does when she's going to argue with me, or when she thinks she's right and I need to learn something.

"You deserve more," she says stubbornly.

My stomach drops, an unpleasant pitch that sends the three beers I've had sloshing in a dramatic, not good kind of way. I reach past her and push open the door, my eyes locked on hers.

Pull her tight to me and lift her, just a little. Without hesitating, she wraps her legs around me, letting me carry her.

It feels right, somehow.

This girl has always felt right, in a way that is hard for me to define or quantify.

The room is lit by a few candles and a lamp by the bed—a queen-sized bed covered in a dark spread and fluffy pillows. My sketch pad and pens are sitting on the side table, waiting like I left them there earlier in the day. Books are scattered on her dresser with a small, carved box and a few mysterious, girly-looking bottles. An oversized desk is pushed against the wall overlooking the window, and her computer sits on one side, my work shit and notebooks on the other.

There are small ropes wrapped around the bedposts that make me grin, and our shoes and clothes are lining the walk-in closet.

The walls, though. They snag and hold my attention.

It's something that took me almost four months to figure out. Even now, Peyton is quiet and almost secretive. She doesn't share herself naturally, and there is very little that is more intrinsic to who she is than her art.

But she is fantastic. Where I prefer ink and charcoals, Pey likes watercolors and the camera.

The walls are a work of art. And a tribute to us. Pictures of me, on stage, smoking outside Keegans, blowing on my hands. One is in a field, and I remember when she took it. We had gone camping, just the two of us and a shitty little tent that we found out had a hole in it. I'm crouched next to a fire, and smiling at her.

I told her I loved her on that trip, after we got rained on and stumbled, cursing, through the storm. Thunder had been so loud, so fucking close, and she had stopped, tipped her head back, and twirled.

Fucking twirled in the rain, dancing in it like a child.

I fucked her in the field, thunder and rain all around us, her body running with water, and whispered those three little words while she shuddered and came.

There are more. Her in my bed, asleep. Us at Barrie's, on New Year's. Me and Scott singing. Us in a park and on our shitty couch, and the back of the truck, and a starscape.

Our whole fucking story is spread over the walls, in brilliant color and haunting black and white.

"Fish," I murmur, and she makes a small noise.

"You like it?" she asks, her hands twisting together nervously, and I walk her backward, until she hits the wall and the picture of me grinning in the snow rattles. She gasps when I push against her, my dick rubbing at her through the layers of clothing.

"I love it," I whisper against her ear. "I love you."

She purrs, a soft noise of satisfaction and rolls her hips. Pleasure shoots through me, and I groan against her lips. "You know moving is exhausting as fuck, right?"

She nips at my lower lip, kisses me, and grins. Pulls back. "Go lay down," she murmurs.

I arch an eyebrow and she smirks.

My shirt hits the floor and I toe off my shoes and shove down my shorts before I sprawl across the bed, propped on my elbows as I watch her.

She ties my ankles first, and I drop back, grinning.

Peyton loves games. She's sweet and proper outside our bedroom. She likes wearing her artistic edge in her clothing and the hair she cut recently, the gauges in her ears and nose piercing. But she's a sweet girl, for all that. Polite, and considerate.

But she's a demanding bitch in the bedroom. And she loves to play dominance games. It's not hardcore shit—neither of us have the bent for true D/s—but sex is a game. One mixed with pain and control and exhibition. It's why she likes being loud when she knows Scott is home, why I can finger fuck her in a bar, or on a crowded city bus. It's hot as fuck, and I'm just kinky enough that I fucking fly on it.

She kisses me once when my hands are tied, and shoves a pillow under my head so I don't have to crane to see her.

Whatever game we're playing, she wants me to have a good view.

She strips slowly, a coy tease as she sways around the room, coming close for a kiss and brushing her bra-clad breast close to my lips before pulling away and shimmying out of her jean shorts.

She's naked and smooth and wet beneath them, and my dick jerks as I strain against the ties.

I'm not going anywhere.

It might all be a game, and I might love to play it, but I'm also not under any delusions about Peyton's seriousness when she comes to play.

"You're tired, right, baby?" she coos, stretching out alongside me. Close, but not close enough. "So you relax. Watch."

My mouth goes dry as she leans her head against my shoulder, her hand dropping down to squeeze her tit. Her back arches a little, and her eyes go glassy as her fingers circle and circle, teasingly light before pinching a nipple and tugging, and her body goes bow-tight against me, her back arching as she moans. Her free hand is trailing down her belly, and I watch it with avid hunger as it smoothes over her soft stomach, the pale, freckled skin, down to her pretty pussy. She whimpers when she brushes her clit, and I swallow. "Does that feel good, sweetheart? Do you feel good?"

"So good," she groans, her fingers sliding along her folds. Her hips are moving, and I'm not sure she's even aware of it as she teases us both. "So wet."

"Show me," I demand, yanking at my ties. "Come here and let me lick that sweet pussy."

She laughs, and the noise turns choked and broken as she slides two fingers deep, her thumb pressed against her clit as she fucks herself. Her head is pressed against my shoulder, digging in, and I can smell her hair and sex. The sound of her fingers sliding in and out of her, the fucking sight of it as her moves become frantic, desperate, her hips churning against her fingers, and she screams, a long, low scream that echoes through our room as she comes.

She's so fucking perfect.

"Don't tease, baby. Let me fuck you."

She twists her head a little, smiling at me sleepily, and her body convulses as she slides her fingers free. Brings them up between us.

"Fucking hell, Peyton," I groan, watching her lick her fingers clean. I'm so hard it hurts, and she's laughing when she kisses me. Licking into her mouth, catching the taste of her on her lips, it's almost like going down on her.

"Thought you were tired," she whispers.

"If you don't fuck me, I swear to god, I will beat your ass red."

"Promise?" she breathes, and I groan.

Curse as she rolls to straddle me. My dick sliding into her wet heat will never be old. Will never be anything short of fucking amazing. I groan and rasp out, "Fuck me, perfect girl."

Her eyes flash and she moves, riding me hard, until I'm cursing and she's crying out with every move, her whole body tight above mine, and then I'm coming, and she screams, her body jerking against mine, clenching tight.

We fall asleep like that. Wrapped up in each other, sticky with sweat and sex and completely fucking in love. Convinced nothing could ever go wrong or change what we have.

Chapter 20: After

Feet ache, pain so familiar

It is almost unfelt.

As she slips on tiptoes,

To a song she cannot sing,

Through eggshells and jagged edges.

And she never realized

The relief that could be found

In dancing through life to a tune

few could hear, in combat boots and

A smile.

(Rike's poems to Peyton)

It takes almost a month for my parents to realize I'm in Nashville. Brody vanishes one Sunday afternoon, and comes back to his downtown, high-rise apartment with its black, modern furniture and clean lines, spitting mad in the way only our father was ever able to achieve.

He's quietly furious, grabbing a beer from the fridge and tossing the cap while he stalks through the apartment. I'm curled in a corner of the couch, leafing through one of the sketchbooks Rike sent home with me, and I eye my baby brother while he paces.

Brody is the youngest of my three siblings, and the one I've always been closest to. He isn't quite the black sheep that I have been, but where Cassidy went to law school and Sean joined Daddy's campaign, Brody joined the Marines. He's filled me in on everything I've missed with him, and I'm so proud of him. He's made a good life in military intel, and if he ever chooses to leave, he can make a better life for himself as a civilian. And he did it without the help of our parents.

He never bought into the political machine life that our parents created, and he never appreciated how they pushed aside my problems to take the next Senate seat.

But we were kids, and kids can't do much to protect themselves.

Maybe that's why I loved Rike. What drew me to him. He was another broken child forgotten by the people who were supposed to care for him.

"Want to storm around and break shit, or do you want to tell me what's wrong?" I drawl.

Brody gives me a dark look, and I smirk. Because he might be all grown up and a badass, but he' still my baby brother. I cross my arms. "Spit it out."

"Mom and Dad want to have a family dinner."

"Fuck," I mutter.

He laughs, and nods. "Exactly. Better find something appropriate to wear."

I snarl a curse, and he snorts. "I wonder if I could wear the leather skirt and my skull and crossbones shirt. I wore that last time. Bonus points for wardrobe reappearances."

Brody's eyebrows shoot up. "You remember that?"

"What?" I ask, flipping my sketchbook back open.

"Wearing that outfit. It was the day Rike met them. Do you remember?"

I stare at him, confusion crowding me. I don't. I don't remember anything about Rike meeting my parents, or why on earth I ever thought that was a good idea. I shake my head helplessly and he sighs. The anger drains away and he comes to the couch, brushing my legs as he drops down. I reach out and snag his beer.

It's still weird that my baby brother can legally drink.

"Do you feel up to it?"

"To seeing Mom and Dad? Fuck no. But I suppose I need to. I can't avoid them forever."

He shrugs. "You were doing a pretty damn good job of doing it before this shit." I wrinkle my nose at him and he laughs. "Fine. This weekend?"

"Ok," I say quietly.

"Good. You want the little Chinese place tonight?" he asks, pushing to his feet. I nod and yawn as he pads into the kitchen to order takeout and set up the dreaded dinner with my parents.

I really will have to go shopping before Saturday.

***

Brody and I play a game, every night while the news plays quietly in the background. It doesn't really have a name, and he would say it's nothing at all, but it is.

It always starts the same.

"Do you remember when you were going to senior prom, and Dad set you up with Tripp Harris?"

I roll my eyes. "How could I forget that? It was awful. Tripp spent weeks trying to talk me into going and Mom bought that hideous dress and then I blew it off—went to the cabin with Lacy and a few other girls. A couple guys. Dad was so fucking pissed when I got home."

Brody grins. "You should have seen him in the two days before you came home. I've seen Dad mad, but I don't think it's ever been that bad."

I shrug. Grin. "He could have called the cops. There was nothing stopping him from that. It was his choice to keep shit quiet to protect the campaign."

Brody's smile slips, and I shift. "Do you remember when you came to Knoxville for the first time to visit me?" I ask.

This is where the game is actually played. When I can get my brother to tell me things I don't know, filling in the events of the years that are still a black hole. The journals have helped so much. I feel like I know who Rike and Scott are. Instead of two strangers who were trying to share my life, they've become two friends who are important for very different reasons. Lindsay—I twist, shaking my head. I can't think about Linds without wanting to cry.

Can't imagine a girl as brilliant and beautiful and alive trapped in a wheelchair.

I shake the melancholy and listen to Brody spin out the story that was mine, and try to ignore the pull of the three people I called family.

* * *

He's been trying to get in touch with me. I can't talk to him, can't hear his voice without hearing it hoarse and broken as he came inside me. And I can't believe I was stupid enough to let that happen.

He texts a lot—more than I think Brody suspects, although he knows some of it. And I told Rike before I left Austin where I was going and that I would be back. But it's been almost a month, and nothing has changed. I know more, but it's secondhand knowledge, the kind that comes from hearing about something instead of experiencing it.

I know he wants me home. But so far, Rike has respected my boundaries.

Rike: *What did you do today?*

Me: *Brody took me to a clothing store I used to love, and I bought a couple outfits. We're having dinner with my parents this weekend, so I thought it was warranted.*

Rike: *You promised me you wouldn't see them without me.*

Me: *I don't remember making that promise. Besides, it's harmless. Nothing will happen.*

There is a long pause, and then he sends a short response.

Rike: *Fine.*

I stare at the phone for a long minute, waiting for something else, but there isn't anything. So he's mad, and I get to deal with my parents.

This week is looking better and better. I grab my notebook and crawl into bed.

I don't write poetry often—despite it being something I love, I don't think I'm very good at it. But as I stare at the blank page, the words start coming. And I write.

***

Brody glances at me as we walk up the paved walkway to my parents' overly large house. He arches an eyebrow. "You ready, princess?"

I make a face and nod at him. He grins and shoves open the door, giving the housekeeper a quick kiss on the cheek before he yells, "Ma! Dad! We're here."

I swallow my laugh and follow him more slowly, hugging Maria before venturing deeper into the house.

It looks exactly like I remember. A house that could fit so easily in a magazine, the décor and pictures chosen to reflect who we are as a family rather than what we love. My nose wrinkles in annoyance, but there is no denying that the familiarity, so fucking rare these days, is comforting.

Brody is in the formal dining room, talking to my mother and Cassidy while Mom fiddles with a centerpiece of brilliant red roses. Her expression, when she finally looks at me, is confusing. There's a flash of guilt and concern, and then it smoothes back into the bland polite smile she perfected years ago.

"Peyton. You look"—her gaze skims over my tight red sundress. It's vintage, with wide, white straps and an oversized white bow. It's almost demure. It would be, if I had buttoned all the buttons up the sweetheart neckline. Her lip tighten—"interesting."

I smile, too sweet, "You look like you just stepped off the campaign trail. So I guess we're both the same as we were yesterday."

"Maybe don't start fighting before we sit down to dinner, Peyton?" Cassidy says sharply. I ignore her. I've been doing that since before high school so it's not terribly difficult to continue the trend now.

"Where is Dad?" I ask as Maria begins carrying in our dinner. I shift, look at Mom.

"He'll be here soon," she says stiffly. With that familiar cold displeasure.

She might be a good little campaigner, and do everything he needs in public, but Mom hasn't ever appreciated the time commitments and how often she was left behind for it.

He lied to her too, when he decided to run for office. He promised that we would stay close, that nothing in our family would change. I think that's why I hate him so much. I never told Rike that. But once upon a time, before politics and that fucking elusive Senate seat, Dad was a good dad. Attentive. Mom was cool, but she wasn't cold.

That changed. Almost overnight.

I shove the thought aside, and follow Maria into the kitchen where I grab a plate of garlic chicken. She gives me a small smile.

"Really, Peyton, that's her job."

"And I'm helping. You understand getting help on a job, right, Cass?"

She flushes, and slams her glass down.

"Ah, here it is. The tension has arrived. Good times," Brody deadpans. "Where are Sean and Lily?" There's a moment of quiet, and then Brody groans. "Really? She's gone already? But this one was only six months!"

"Maybe don't bring it up. I know you're still catching up but he wasn't expecting it."

My older brother is a serial cheater. How he can't expect the women he dates to leave him, I'll never understand. The bickering continues as we sit down and Mom waits patiently for Maria to serve her before we all make our plates. She glances at me, a potato speared on her fork.

"Peyton, have you gotten a dress for the gala next week? I have a few that would look lovely on you."

My stomach lurches and I drop my fork, reaching for my wine instead. "What gala?"

"The one next week. The hospital is having it and your father is the keynote speaker. He expects you to attend."

I don't believe this. Except, I do. It's a classic move for my father. I sit back with my wine and my mother's brow furrows. "Eat, Peyton."

"Not hungry," I snap.

Cassidy smiles, a sharp brittle thing, "That's normal, though, right?"

The dig at my eating disorder stings.

"Shut the fuck up, Cass," Brody snaps, and I jerk to my feet.

Big hands close over my hips, pulling me back into a broad chest and the scent of soap and smoke. His beard brushes over my bare shoulder as he kisses my cheek, and then he glances up. At my family.

"Mrs. Collins," he says coldly.

Mom is eyeing Rike like he's a vagrant who wandered into her pristine house, and I have to swallow my giggle.

"I told you that Peyton is my responsibility. Mine to keep safe and keep healthy. That means I keep her the fuck away from you because you're fucking toxic." I gasp, twisting to stare at him. He's watching my mother, loathing in his eyes. "She's not yours anymore, not to manipulate. Stay the fuck away from her."

Mom stands, her cheeks red and her hands shaking. I don't think I've ever seen her this furious. "You have no right to even be here."

He smiles, a lazy arrogant thing that makes my heart pound. "I have the only right."

And then he escorts me out of my parent's house.

Chapter 21: Before

Scott is actually sitting on the new couch when I emerge from my bedroom. Lindsay and Peyton are in the kitchen, and I glance at my best friend in a rare moment without either present. "You good, dude?" I ask.

His eye flick to mine and I'm startled by what I see there. He looks peaceful. Content. That's a look I'm not used to seeing on Scotty. It's almost disturbing.

"I'm good," he says, and the last band of unease loosens. Because it's going to work. This. Us together, with the women we fucking adore. It's going to work. He grins suddenly. "Broke in the new bed, huh?"

"You and Linds didn't exactly go to sleep after bedtime prayers," I deadpan.

He laughs, a satisfied noise. "Well, she did say 'Oh *God*' a lot, so I think that should totally count."

"Can you two behave for like, five minutes?" Lindsay asks grumpily, slipping past me to nestle against Scott on the couch.

"Where the hell is the fun in that?" Scott asks, kissing her head absently. "You got class today?"

She nods. "We both have our schedules on the fridge."

I frown at Scott. "When the fuck did we become dudes with schedules on the fridge?"

"When you fell for a siren in a bar," he shoots back. "Quit bitching. I like sex on the regular."

"Like that was ever an issue," Lindsay snorts, and he smacks her lightly on the back of the head. Peyton ambles up with a cup of coffee and two pieces of toast. I steal one and she growls when I drift too close to her coffee. I laugh softly and kiss her cheek instead. She's not a friendly person in the morning, especially before coffee.

"You need a ride today?" I ask, and she shakes her head, pulls the coffee away from her lips long enough to murmur, "Linds will take me."

"When are your parents getting into town?" Lindsay asks, and Peyton goes tense under my arm. I glance at her and she's glaring at her best friend like Lindsay just stabbed her dog.

"Fish?" I ask, softly.

She breathes out a curse and twists to look at me. "Tomorrow. My parents and youngest brother will be here tomorrow. Dad has a fundraiser. I've been invited."

My head is spinning and I take a step back. I'm conscious suddenly of the tattoos tracing up and down my arms, the eyebrow ring, too-long hair. and beard.

I'm a fucking tattooed hillbilly rock star, and not even a good one. Why the hell is it surprising that she doesn't want to share that with her parents?

It's not. But it stings. More than I want to admit, it stings. Because I thought we were past this. I thought we were in a good fucking place. I've been waiting for six months for the shoe to drop, and I had convinced myself it wouldn't.

It just fucking did.

"I see," I say, simply.

Then I turn and stalk out of the room, slamming the door behind me on her protests and Scott's sharp voice calling Lindsay off.

It doesn't fucking matter. She'll have a pretty excuse, some logical reason why I should swallow her hiding her parents from me. But it doesn't matter. The door opens behind me, but I don't stop walking.

"Rike, *stop*!" she snaps, yanking on my arm, and jerking me around to face her. "Let me fucking explain."

"Why? It's shit I've heard before. I don't really want to rehash, and you'll be late." I force a smile. "You can't be late on your first day of class, Fish. Get going."

She stares at me for a long moment before a disbelieving laugh bubbles up. "Is that really all you've got? You'll be late, get going? Are you fucking serious?"

"What do you want me to say?" I snap. "Your parents are coming into town. You hid that from me. You're embarrassed. I get it. He's a politician and she's a perfect political wife, and I'm a tattooed high school drop out with a juvie record. I get it. I'm not take-you-home-to-Mom material. But fuck, Peyton. It hurts a little."

She's pale, her freckles standing out against her white skin as she stares at me with wide eyes. "Is that really what you think of me?"

"What did you expect me to think?"

"I expected you to trust me. That I love you and if—" My eyebrows raise, and she scowls "When I choose to keep something from you, it's for a good fucking reason. I expect you to know that."

I shrug. "You might be expecting too much, sugar."

She takes a step back, hurt pooling in her bright eyes. I hate seeing that look on her face. Hate that I put it there. But this is one time I can't back down.

I give her a final look, a small smile. "Go to class, Fish. you'll be late."

Then I walk away, and try to think of anything but how much this hurts.

***

The tattoo I'm supposed to be drawing is for a client. A giant fucking back piece—eagles and fish and some other tribal nonsense, all done in dark band and artistic, vague, half-formed images.

It should look amazing if a little bit hipster and pretentious for my taste.

"That is not tribal art," Scotty says, dropping beside me. The breeze of his arrival ruffles my sheet of paper, and I flick a look at him. There is so much I could say here, but why? It doesn't change anything.

"You need to let her explain."

"When did you start taking her side in shit, dude?" I snap, refocusing on the art.

"When you fell in love with her. She fucked up by keeping it from you. I'm not denying that. But she deserves a chance to explain why. She's not an idiot and she loves you."

"And we all self-sabotage," I say

"Peyton isn't trying to get out of this. If she was, she wouldn't have moved in and built a shrine to your relationship. She's in this. So let her explain why the fuck she's hiding her parents. We aren't the only ones who came into this with baggage.

He rises and I glance at him. "You don't have a session today."

"I'm not here for me," he says, staring back at me.

I swallow the snappy comeback, and nod once. Turn back to the sketch.

It's a koi, a bright red fish with blue scales gleaming almost iridescently along its sides, twisted on its own tail. It's all soft and sweet and I know it's for her.

Staci come up beside me, and peers at it. "Good work. You adding it to your portfolio? "

"I don't know," I say. She glances at me, her gaze assessing and sharp.

It's vaguely disconcerting, and I know why. Staci took a chance on me. I wasn't going to take her up on her offer. But I love the shop. I love the sound of the tattoo machine, and the stories behind the art, even the stupid as fuck pieces that kill my soul a little. I like getting to know the clients, and seeing the excitement in their eyes when they see my sketches.

I even like that it hurts. Peyton laughs and calls me a sadistic masochist. She might be on to something.

Staci taking a chance on me gave me the choice to be good at something. Something that allowed me to still be creative. And I didn't want to let her down.

"You need to be focused," she says quietly. "This shit we do—it's for real. It lasts forever. So we give the client every bit of our attention while we're here. I don't know what happened with Peyton, but you need to leave it at the door."

I nod, and tuck the sketch of the koi aside. Force a smile for my boss and straighten. "I'll have it done in a few hours."

I get lost in the art, my mind racing as I sketch, and despite Staci's admonition, I'm struggling to figure out how the hell this happened. What she thought could be gained by hiding her parents coming to town.

Peyton and her folks don't get along. They haven't since her last stint in rehab for the anorexia. I know that. I've read her own words, seen the pictures.

I know she was miserable being forced into the political daughter mold.

But I also know she's here on their dime. She goes to school, pays rent and her bills, buys food—all with money they provide. She might hate the hold they have on her, and she might not go home to dance to their tune, but she depends on them.

Is that why she's hiding me?

I huff out a sigh, and shove the thoughts aside, focusing on the design. She can explain it. I owe her that much—and we live together. It's not like I can avoid her forever.

***

Lindsay is home when I get in from the shop, and she gives me that knowing smirk she does so well that annoys the fuck out of me. I like the girl—I really do, and not just because she's Peyton's best friend and Scott's girlfriend; I like her for her own merits—

but she's got a cocky attitude about shit, especially when she thinks I'm wrong about something.

Which is often.

I grit my teeth. "Is she here?"

"Shower. You sure you're ready for this, Rike? Her parents are no joke."

I ignore that. Lindsay is the only one who has a normal family. People who support and love without conditions. People who stuck around.

Sometimes I wonder if she's with us just out of curiosity, and then I remind myself that thinking that is fucking shitty, and that she really cares about Scott.

"Thanks," I mutter.

The bathroom door is closed, and I eye it briefly. The bed is still unmade, and I wonder if we'll get back to where we were last night.

We will. This is a hiccup, but we've had those before. We'll be fine, because we have to be fine.

The shower turns off, and I hear music blaring for a moment before she cuts it off and emerges, wrapped in a towel and steam and water droplets still clinging to her shoulders.

She eyes me briefly, and ruffles her wet hair. "You need to change."

"Why?" I ask, keeping my tone even.

"Because we're meeting my parents," she says. "Dinner at Ruth's Chris."

I cross my arms, and study her coldly. "Is there a dress code for this shit?"

"Something you didn't just pull a shift in," she says, still buried in her closet, and I huff. It finally sinks in that I'm pissed, because she emerges from her closet and frowns at me. "What the hell is wrong now?"

"You suddenly want me to meet your parents."

"I never didn't want you to meet them, asshole. I didn't want you to have to deal with their shit. But it's a big deal to you, and I get it. So we'll go."

She tosses a dress on the bed and glares at me. "I wasn't going to go. I didn't keep it from you because I was planning to see them without you. I kept it from you because it doesn't matter. Like not telling you I put gas in the truck and bought a candy bar on the way home. So fucking irrelevant."

I stare at her and it's hard as fuck to swallow my irritation and all the protests. I shake my head and strip out of the grungy shirt I'm wearing, stalking into the bathroom and turning on the shower.

We don't fight. Maybe that's why I'm struggling with this so hard. Scott and Lindsay fight constantly—it's their form of foreplay. But we don't. We never have. Being with Peyton is easy. Even when one of us is being a moody artist, it's easy.

When I step out of the shower, she's in the bathroom, leaning into the mirror as she does her makeup. She's barely dressed, only a strapless white bra with black lace details and a matching thong. Her gaze meets mine in the mirror, and I see apology flickering there before she refocuses.

We're going to do it that way then.

I slip past her silently and we're both quiet as we dress.

***

We take the truck, and Peyton sits on her side of the cab in tense silence. She looks fucking amazing, in a tiny dark red shirt with a skull on it and a tight little leather skirt. The neckline wraps around her neck, leaving her shoulders bare, and the skirt ends mid-thigh, exposing a mouthwatering length of leg. I'm itching to run my hand up the smooth skin, under that flirty skirt to the tiny panties I know she's wearing.

We didn't fool around when getting ready. We barely spoke.

"I didn't have a family, Peyton," I say abruptly. "I didn't do family shit, and I don't have family for you to meet. The only family I have is Scott, and I've never tried to keep him from you."

"Because Scott is someone you want to have in your life. Because Scott isn't an asshat." I arch an eyebrow and she snorts. "Ok, but he's your asshat."

"And these are yours," I say softly.

She shakes her head. "You and Scott and Linds are my family. Not them. But. You'll see."

I reach for her hand and squeeze it gently in my own. "I just want to know where you come from, Fish."

She make a choked little noise that worries me, but we're pulling up to the steakhouse. She takes a deep breath as the valet approaches, and I glance at her.

"Come on," she says. "Let's get it over with."

She shoves the door open and slides down without waiting for me, and I follow suit, taking the valet ticket and slipping it into my pocket while following her inside.

"Party for Senator Collins," she says to the hostess. The girl nods, snapping to attention as she leads us deeper into the restaurant.

They're sitting at a table in a back corner, surrounded by other empty tables. A man in a black suit eyes me as we approach, but doesn't try to stop us.

Peyton's shoulders are back, and her smile is stiff as she pauses, hands on the back of the chair. "Mom. Dad. Good to see you."

The senator is a tall man with broad shoulders, sharp eyes, and Pey's freckles. Her mother is softer, curvy with a wide-eyed innocent smile that screams fake, and a power suit that would make Hilary Clinton jealous. And they're watching Peyton with something like disgust in their eyes. Shock. That's what it is.

"Well. That is certainly a different look, sweetheart."

Peyton touches her hair and gives a smile. "Like it, Ma?"

"Not particularly," comes the stiff reply.

"Pity," Peyton coos, sugar sweet and I swallow a laugh. She tucks her hand into my arm and tugs me forward a step or two. "I'd like to introduce you to my boyfriend, Rike Johnson."

Their eyes swing to me, and the younger dude lets out a startled laugh. "Damn, Pey. Did you pick him to piss them off?"

"Fuck off, Brody," she says lazily, and for the first time since we arrived, a real grin tugs at her lips as she flicks a glance at her brother. He laughs, a soft noise that reminds me of her, and some of the tension eases from her shoulders. She pulls a chair out and sits, and motions for me to do the same, putting me between her and her brother, away from her parents.

Who are still staring at me like I'm a devil bent on pillaging their daughter's virtue.

"Nice to meet you," I say with a small smile.

They stare, and the senator blinks once, then focuses on his daughter. "What the hell is this?"

"My boyfriend."

"No." He doesn't even argue. Just a flat no, like she should care about what this prick has to say.

"Do you think we can order drinks before we start in on how Pey has fucked up her life?" she says, and my heart hurts. She doesn't ever change her tone. It's classic defensive Peyton.

A puzzle piece of the enigmatic girl slides into place. I glance at her, at the pleasant smile, and I get it, suddenly.

"What the hell are you trying to prove with this?" Collins hisses.

"I'm not trying to prove anything. It was never about that." She turn to me. "What do you want to drink?"

A very petty part of me wants to ask for a beer just to fuck with her folks, but her big eyes are pleading and desperate, and I remember suddenly that

she is only here because I threw a bitch fit this
morning.

"The Talbot pinot noir," I say, flashing a
quick smile at the hovering waitress. She gets the rest
of the orders, and scurries away.

The senator is looking at me instead of his
daughter now, which has to be an improvement. I
push up my sleeves and his eyes tighten at the sight of
the colorful tattoos tracing up my left arm. I meet the
hostile smile with my own. "Good to meet you, sir.
Peyton has told me a lot about you."

"Note that he didn't say it was good shit,
Dad," Brody says.

"Well, I do try to avoid lying. My mama
raised me well," Peyton deadpans and Brody laughs,
shaking his head.

"We didn't realize you were dating, Peyton,"
Mary Anne says.

She leans back, and I feel her hand on my
back, a steady pressure. I don't know if it's for me or
her, but it's soothing. "We've been together for over

six months. And before you ask—I'm not hiding shit. I'm living my life. You haven't bothered to ask or visit, so excuse me if you aren't up to date on who and what is important in my life."

"You made it clear when you left for UT that you didn't want us involved in your life," Mary Anne says stiffly.

"And you've always been so fucking good at listening to what I want, right? That's why Dad first ran for office. Because you totally listened when I said I didn't want anything to do with his political circus."

Mary Anne makes a dismissive noise and waves a hand at Collins. "You deal with her. You're the one who thinks her being at the benefit is a good idea."

"She lives here. How the hell will it look if she lives here and doesn't show up to support the campaign?" Collins says evenly.

"Give it up, Dad. I'm not coming to the fundraiser. I'm done doing the political daughter shit.

I'm here, now. As your daughter to let you meet Rike. Now do you want to focus on that or should we go?"

The senator and Peyton glare at each other for a long tense moment, and then he huffs. "Will you consider it?"

"Will you drop it if I say yes?" He nods and she shrugs. "Sure. I'll consider it."

Brody snorts and I turn my attention on Peyton's younger brother.

He's got the same red hair, just a few shades darker, a wide grin, and mischievous eyes that are instantly likable. He's the only one in her family she ever talks about. She likes her young, wild brother. I think he's the only reason she ever goes home—even on her abbreviated visits.

"Tell me about yourself. What do your parents do?" Collins says as the waitress puts our drinks down. She takes our order and then scurries away and I have to face the question.

I shrug. "My mother was addicted to crack. We bounced around with her pimp for a while. She overdosed when I was six and I landed in the system. My father—well, he's never been part of the picture."

He blinks at me, and I stare, my face blank.

No one is ever completely comfortable with me dropping the info like that. And this guy—he doesn't want me anywhere near his daughter to start with.

"Were you adopted, then?" Mary Anne asks.

"Nope. I was in and out of group homes and foster families until I aged out. Spent six months in juvie when I was fourteen for assault. When I turned eighteen, my best friend and I had a little bit of money saved up, so we got a place and that was that."

She looks startled, and I smile. "Not exactly the pretty picture you wanted, right?"

"How serious is this?" Collins asks, his gaze on Peyton. He's gone back to pretending I don't exist.

"We just moved in together, Dad. Pretty fucking serious."

"You know he's using you, right? For your trust fund."

"Fuck, Dad," Brody sighs.

"What's shocking, Dad? The fact that someone wants me or the fact that I'm not playing the dutiful daughter?" she snaps.

"I don't need your daughter's money, Senator. Frankly, I've tried to convince her to quit using it to pay for rent. I make more than enough to support us both. I'm with her because I love her."

"Excuse me if I choose to not trust a violent felon," he says coldly.

"That's what everyone focuses on. My violent crimes. Peyton asked, you know. Why. The why is more important than the what, and I'd do it again. Every fucking time."

The table is quiet and then Brody asks softly, "Why?"

"His best friend. Scott was being abused. He'd kept it quiet for a while, and pulled the attention from the other kid in the house. He made himself a target to protect them, and kept it from Rike because he knew how Rike would react."

I close my eyes, and lean back. Let her tell the story.

"One afternoon, Rike shows up at the foster home. They haven't seen each other in months—just emails to keep in touch and to make sure the other is safe. They're all each other has, right? So he shows up at this foster home. It was a bad time—Scott was home with the bastard while the other kids were out and he'd managed to piss the guy off, not that it's hard, you know. And Rike walks in on him beating the shit out of Scott. Scott's covered in blood and piss, barely fucking conscious, and Rike—well, he's smart. He knows it's been happening for a while. He can read bruises like most people can read the paper. And he lost it. Attacked the guy with a glass bottle he found on the table. By the time they got Rike off the dude, he'd carved his face up and beaten him to a pulp. The guy spent a month in the hospital before he was tossed in jail. Rike should have gotten a fucking medal. Instead, he got six months and probation, and wasn't allowed near Scott for two years."

The longest two years of our life. We did what they said—mostly because I wouldn't risk Scott being moved to another county. We made it work. And by then, we were so close to aging out, freedom was almost something we could taste.

We rode it out, waited until we aged out and put it behind us, as much we could.

It's hard to forget something that put scars on your soul and body.

"Maybe, Dad, you should find out why you're judging someone before you decide to write them off," she says softly.

"You haven't given us a lot of reason to trust your judgement, Pey," he counters.

"Enough," Brody snaps. He glances between his sister and father, scowling. "We didn't meet here to fight. Dad, do you think you could manage to get through dinner without judging every decision she makes? You don't have to like it, but she's not tied to

the campaign, so it's not hurting you and she's happy.
That does matter a little bit." He doesn't wait for an
answer. Turns to me, and forces a small smile. "So,
aside from beating up abusers, what do you do with
yourself, Rike?"

I eye him but he doesn't look like he's trying
to find a way to trip me up. He looks curious and
patient and hopeful. He's throwing me a bone.

"I'm a songwriter," I say, flashing a smile.
"And I'm apprenticing with a local tattoo artist."

Brody's eyes widen and a smile twitches his
lips. As her mother starts in on the problems with
dating a degenerate, Brody shakes his head. "Good
luck, man."

Chapter 22: After

Never anyone's only.
She said that, drunk and sad and
I wanted to scream.
My first thought is yours. my smile and
Dreams and pleasure. I see you in every
sunrise and teardrop and birdsong.
Not my only.
Only my everything.
(Rike's poems to Peyton)

He almost dumps me into the truck. His truck. "What are you even doing here?" I demand, and he slams the door in my face. I huff a sigh, twisting in my seat to stare at him as he climbs in the truck.

"What are you doing here?" I demand again, and he leans across the console, catching me by the back of the next and kissing me. It's hot and hungry and forceful. There is no soft request; it's a demand.

It always has been with him.

I bite his lip and his hand clenches in my hair, jerking just a little, riding a delicious line of pain, his tongue in my mouth, twisting and stroking.

"I should spank your ass for that shit. You can't go there alone. They're horrible for you. Promise me, Peyton?"

He never uses my full name, and it shocks me enough that I nod. He sighs, and sits back. "I'm not fucking you in my truck in your parent's driveway. I love you too much for that. So put your seatbelt on and let's go, because I do need to fuck you. Soon."

Why the hell does that blunt, crude admission turn me on so fucking much?

I pull on my seatbelt, and he squeals out of my parent's driveway.

"You don't like them," I say after a few minutes.

His gaze turns to me, pure disbelief, and I swallow hard. "No fucking shit, Pey."

He drives for about five minutes, and then jerks the truck off the road, onto a dirt road that serves as a driveway to an old, little used farm. "What are we doing?" I ask, nervously.

"Your brother's house is thirty minutes from here, and my hotel is farther than that. And I can't wait that long to fuck you," he says matter-of-factly, stopping the truck. He glances at me, the look hot and invasive. "You look fucking amazing, Fish."

Then he's out of the truck and I have just a few seconds to decide. If this is what I want. If Rike is who I want. Then the door pops open, and his hands are on my legs, pulling me around to face him. He nudges them open and settles against me, hugging me. His shoulders relax as he clings to me. "I've missed you, Fish. So fucking much."

I don't know how to respond to that. Except... "I missed you too," I confess quietly. The truth. How can I miss someone I barely know, someone who shouldn't matter to me? But should or not, he does.

He matters so much.

Rike looks up at me, his blue eyes hungry. "I want you. But it's your choice. It's always been your choice." Something crosses his eyes and he smirks at me, a crooked little boy grin. "Stay or go?" he murmurs.

A shudder runs through me, and my body goes soft and pliant, my panties wet. I've heard him say that before and it was hot.

"Stay," I whisper.

His eyes flare and then he's pulling me down, and I slide down his body, against this thick erection. He groans and I smile, just barely resisting the urge to wrap my legs around his waist and grind against him.

Instead, I keep sliding down, until I'm on my knees. "Peyton," he says hoarsely.

I unzip his pants, and my hands are on him. Stroking over the silky skin. His dick kicks in my hand and I giggle, sliding his pants and boxers aide. He has two tattoos, trailing down that sexy v that makes my mouth water. A pair of dragons in mid-flight. I lean down and kiss one, my tongue licking over it, and he grunts, thrusting a little. I pull back and he curses. "Don't tease, baby. Let me fuck your pretty little mouth."

My hand comes up and cups his balls, tugging gently, and he grunts. I lick over the matching dragon. "Dirty girl. You fucking love this. Want me to beg? Because I'm begging. Do it, babe. Suck my dick." I take his cock deep, my lips tight around him and his head falls back, hissing, "Fuck, yes, baby."

I whimper as his hands find my hair, and he thrusts gently. "Love that dick, don't you, dirty girl?"

I keep one hand on his cock, and slip the other one down, pulling up my skirt and slipping a hand between my legs.

"Yes," he groans. "Fuck yes, touch yourself, Pey. You're wet, aren't you? So wet. I could fuck you so easy right now, babe."

I scream, shuddering as I come, a combination of the dirty, raspy words, and my fingers, and the fucking crazy high of controlling his pleasure. His hands are on me, jerking me up and I scream again as he buries himself in my pussy.

"Fuck, yes," he groans, pulling back and slamming into me again. He shifts me against the truck, slides a hand between my ass and the door and pulls me into him, meeting each furious thrust. Each one sets off another tiny orgasm, until there is nothing but sensation, and pleasure, and his body and mine.

***

We fuck again when we get to the hotel, against the door while he chants my name like a prayer and plays my body like an instrument. After, I cuddle next to him on the bed, his fingers toying in my hair.

"I want you to come home," he says into the silence.

I squeeze my eyes closed. I knew it was coming, but still—to hear it said so bluntly is like running headlong into a brick wall. I shift, so I'm lying across his chest. The koi on his arm stares up at me through the shield of seaweed and coral, and I study it.

"I love that one," I say. He chuckles, and I prop myself up, glaring at him. "What?"

"You should. It's yours." My mouth falls open and he laughs again. "Why the hell does that surprise you? Half my ink is because of you."

"Tell me," I demand.

He pushes off the bed, and stands naked next to me. I make a small hum of appreciation and Rike laughs again. "Stop. Focus."

With some effort—and a good deal of reluctance—I force my attention from the more interesting bits of his anatomy to the ink he's pointing at.

I'm a patchwork across his body. The pinup girl on his ribcage with her head turned away, and long red hair. The script wrapped around his right wrist. The matching swallows on his back. And the koi, the brilliant tattoo that's captivated me since I woke up in the hospital.

"Why do you call me Fish?" I ask, tracing it.

"People say there's plenty of fish in the sea. I say, fuck you, she was my sea."

My breath catches and I glance up at hm. Let my lips curve into a tiny smile. "Doesn't take mean I'm Sea?"

He shifts, covering me and sliding into me in one move that makes my laugh catch in my throat. Turn into a broken groan.

"Fish sounds better," he whispers, watching me.

I whimper, and he smiles, a smile so fucking beautiful and sad it makes me want to cry. Moves in me, slow and sweet, his lips on my neck and shoulders and lips, whispering sweet, dirty words of love while he makes love to me, until I gasp, my body arching against him as I come apart.

When he comes, a few seconds later, he whispers, so softly, "I love you, Fish."

Chapter 23: Before

The girls are out. Peyton wanted tequila, and after the few hours we spent with her parents, I don't blame her much. I want some painkillers and my bed.

"Was it bad?"

"I won't make her visit her parents again; let's put it that way," I say, scrubbing a hand over my face.

Scotty's quiet for a long minute, and I frown, glancing up at him. "Ever wonder if we were lucky? Our parents were awful, but at least we didn't get stuck with them. We got free."

"Being put in the system isn't free, Scott. It's just in a fucking broken system."

He nods. "Yeah. I know. But we're out now. And at least in the system we found some family.

Maybe not the one we were born with, but family that you choose is just as important. Maybe more, in a way."

I stare at him. "Where the actual fuck is this coming from?"

He shrugs. "Dunno. I guess now that we have the girls—we're our own family. We created something for ourselves that we never had. What would we do if we lost that? If the girls walked away or decided that we aren't good enough as we are?"

I think about Peyton, and her fierce anger with her father, the way she defended me and refused to let him and Mary Anne tear me apart. I think of Lindsay and her good-natured teasing, the way she fights with Scott while pulling him closer. I think of how they both vanished, giving me and him the time to process shit, and how she put together that fucking perfect room, the way they've slipped so effortlessly into our lives, and made it their own.

How Linds will work to get us gigs. How Peyton is so quick to encourage me and Scott to try new things, shit that will make us better. Happier.

"They wouldn't do that," I say hoarsely. Because now I'm thinking about it, and the idea of losing them, even for a little while, is fucking terrifying.

Lindsay isn't mine. She won't ever be, and I don't want her. But the four of us—we're a fucking family. And I hate even the thought of losing that. I glance at my best friend, the brother I never had. "They wouldn't."

"No, brother," he says gently. "They wouldn't."

I stand abruptly and go into my room, grabbing the sketch I did this morning. I extend it to him silently, and his eyes widen. "Yeah?" he says, his gaze flicking up to me.

"I want it to be the anchor piece for my right sleeve."

A smile turns his lips, and he nods. "I like it, dude. It's appropriate and she'd love it. Not that you're going to tell her."

I grin, "Not 'til it's done anyway."

"Secretive bastard," he accuses, and I nod.

There's a knock on the door, and he arches an eyebrow at me silently. We haven't been here long enough that anyone knows where we're at. Staci does, and so does Barrie, but only because that's work. "Did the girls forget their keys?" I ask, walking to the door.

"No. Linds wanted to stop and get hers bedazzled or some shit," he snorts.

I laugh and open the door.

Brody is standing there, his eyes darting around as he hunches forward, his hands tucked into his pockets. He's looking around like he thinks he might be shanked for being here and I have to swallow my laugh. Because I like her brother, and he doesn't know that this is actually a really good neighborhood, as our price range goes.

Poor kid would have a heart attack if he knew where his sister had been slumming before we moved here.

"What are you doing here?" I ask, staring at him.

"Uh, hello, future brother-in-law, yes I would love to come in." From the couch, Scott snorts a laugh, and puts aside his guitar to stand and come to the door.

"Who are you?" he asks without preamble.

"Brody. And you're Scott. Where is Peyton?"

"She went to get alcohol."

Brody laughs. "Dad has that effect on folks, and especially on her."

I nod, and Scott heaves a sigh, grabbing my arm and pulling me aside while Brody steps into the apartment and closes the door behind him.

"What are you doing here, man?" Scott asks.

"You love my sister," he says, looking at me.

I nod, and he grins. "Good. You're good for her. Peyton is different from the rest of us. She's creative and spontaneous and wild. I thought for a long time that she killed that when she played the good little political daughter, but she didn't. And then--she told you about the eating disorder? About rehab?"

I nod and my gut clenches. Because I'll run to the farthest ends of the earth to keep her away from these people. To make sure that she never becomes the shell of the girl she was then.

"It changed her, man. Fucked her up for a long time. She had a hard time letting people in after that. And she quit playing the part, got deeper into her own head and creativity—but I haven't seen the girl I grew up with in years, not the way I saw her tonight. I want you to know that." He shifts and grins. "I saw my sister again, man. And you made that happen. You are bringing her out of her shell. So I don't really give a fuck who you are or what you do or what fucked up past you have hiding. I respect what you did." His gaze darts to Scott, and then back to me, and my best friend shifts.

"So why are you here?" I ask. "I appreciate the vote of confidence and shit but it seems a little excessive."

"I love Peyton. I get her in a way I don't get my brother. But she doesn't need to be anywhere near my parents. They won't ever accept what she wants, because it's not the picture they have in their mind for her. I get where they're coming from—she's the youngest daughter and all that shit. But it's bad for her. And she's self-destructive when shit gets bad. So keep her away. Don't let her come back to this."

I stare at him, startled. "You want me to keep Peyton away from her family?"

"I don't want you to be the reason Peyton comes back to her family. She won't, not on her own. But she loves you and you've never had one. She wants to give to the people she loves, and if she thinks this is something you want, she'll come home just to give you what you never had. And it'll destroy her, and what you two have. No one wants that. Well, I don't. She doesn't. You don't. So do her and yourself a favor and build your life without her family."

"But you love her."

"I do. And I'm going to be around, especially when I get out of college and can cut the apron strings. But in the meantime, I want my sister happy. Do that for me." He stares at me, and his eye aren't amused or laughing. He's dead serious. I nod and his lips twitch into a tired smile. "Thanks man. I--just thanks."

He hugs me, abruptly, and I go stiff, startled. Behind him, Scott is staring, his eyes huge and laughing. Then he steps back and grins at me. "Take care of yourself, Rike."

Chapter 24: After

I want to strip the masks from you,

Until you are as

broken and

Raw and

Vulnerable.

As you leave me.

(Rike's poems to Peyton)

"I need you to come home," he says the next morning. I peer at him over a cup of coffee and he sits down across from me. He's dressed in a pair of loose flannel sleep, pants his chest bare except for ink. And my teeth marks.

I flush, and look away.

"Why?" I ask and his eyebrows rise.

I shake my head, "Why now? What's different about now?"

"Lindsay is being released from the hospital. Scott has talked her into coming home. But she needs her family. She needs you, just as much as she needs him. It's an all or nothing kind of thing."

"So, no pressure, right?" I joke, and he shakes his head.

"No, Pey. This is all the pressure. I'm not going to lie to you about that. Scott and Lindsay are doing worse than we are, and we aren't even living in the same fucking state since you moved in with Brody. We're falling apart. I don't know that Scott'll survive losing Lindsay. I need you to come home, because I can't lose my best friend and the love of my life. And we don't work without all of us."

I reach for him, squeezing his hand. "You don't have to talk me into this, Rike. I'm in this. I know I've been distant. And I'm sorry; I had to be. I had to figure out who I am."

"I know. I'm sorry. I want to give you time—"
He sighs. Shakes his head. "No, I don't. I want to take
you home, lock you in our room, and fuck you until
you can't remember a time when we weren't together.
Until I'm a part of you, so fucking wrapped up in you
that there is no you or me. Just us. That's what I've
wanted since the day you opened your eyes. But I've
given you time and space because I know that what I
wanted wasn't what you needed and I love you too
much to force you into something."

"You aren't," I protest, and he holds up a hand.

"Let me finish, Peyton," he says.

I fall silent, stung just a little. He huffs out a
breath. "I love you. I always will. But I'm not going to
force you into this because I do. Not when you can't
remember loving me. I love you too much for that. I
would walk away and wait for you to come to me. I
would wait for you forever, if I had to. But Lindsay
doesn't have that kind of patience. She never has. We
need you to keep her and our family together. The
only person who matters to me the way you do is
Scott." His gaze is pleading and sad when he finally

lifts those bright blue eyes to look at me. "He's my brother and he's falling apart, Peyton. She's talking about going to her parents' house. About never coming home. He can't—he can't lose her."

I put my coffee down and lean forward, catching his hand in mine. Squeezing it until his gaze finds mine, so desolate and broken.

I did this. I left him. He's not seeing Lindsay leaving Scott, and how that will fall out. He's remembering me leaving him, and how fucking horrible it will be for his best friend to live through that same nightmare.

I hate that I've done that to him.

"Ok, Rike. Let's go home."

Chapter 25: Before

It happens a few weeks before Christmas. We've been playing for increasingly busier crowds. More nights spent in bars and venues we've never been to than in Barrie's. It's caused a bit of a strain with him, but I'm following Scott's lead—this is his dream, and I'll follow wherever he chooses to chase it.

Ever since we played "Perfect Girl," we've been growing. It's opened doors for Scott as a singer and me as a songwriter that neither of us expected. And the girls have cheered us along—Linds has worked almost as hard as Scott to find new venues and bands to open for, anything to get more exposure.

Anytime I wonder about her and how she feels about Scott, I remember that.

"See that guy?" she asks now, almost bouncing in her seat. "Black suit, red tie, looks like Simon Cowell's cuter younger brother?" I crane my head and see the dude she's talking about. The guy has been on his phone all night and Scott scowls in his direction. She raps the table sharply with one finger. "He's with an indie label out of Austin, up scouting talent in Nashville. I got a friend to pass him your demo."

"When did we make a demo?" I wonder, and Lindsay flicks me a longsuffering look. I hold up a hand in surrender.

"So he's interested in the guys?" Peyton says curiously.

"Yeah. So do good tonight." She leans into Scott, kissing him before she hops down and scurries for the bar. Peyton follows. They don't do bars alone, and they know we like a minute alone before we take the stage.

There are nerves in Scott's eyes when I look at him, unexpected nerves, and I lean forward. "Same shit, brother. Sing like we're still at Barrie's."

"We aren't though," he says, blowing out a breath. "This is real."

I nod. "But it's everything we've been working for. So. Embrace the real shit, dude."

"The real shit is risky as hell," he says.

I get it.

It's a risk every time we debut a new song, anytime we do a show anywhere that isn't Barrie's. There's comfort in the familiar old ruts but…"We get to decide who and what we are," I say quietly. Then I stand up and go to where the opening act is winding down, pulling my drumsticks. My koi winks up at me, a brilliant flare of color that grounds me while we ride the crowd's energy.

Scott bounds onto the stage a step ahead of me, and I let out a relieved sigh. The mood has passed and he's ready to perform.

***

"Gentlemen," a smooth voice says behind us. It cuts through Peyton's low murmur and Lindsay's excited chatter as they hug us and we order drinks. The set is over, just, and we're still surrounded by throbbing noise and the energy of the music. And the studio exec is staring at us with a smile on his face.

Real shit is scary as fuck.

"Hey, man," Scott says, disentangling from Lindsay and shaking the guy's hand. "Thanks for being here."

"It was a great set. I had a chance to listen to your demo. I don't think that last song was on it. What was the name?"

"Chosen," I say. Peyton's hand slips in mine and I smile at the dude, a tight, reserved smile, slipping easily into my role of quiet backup to Scott's cocky devil may care disregard "And it's new. We debuted it a few weeks ago."

Apparently, that was after the demo, but whatever.

"I think my bosses would like it. I'd like to arrange a meeting where you boys can play some for them and talk about what kind of future you have. Is that something you think you'd be interested in?"

Scott's tense and still at my side, and the girls seem far away. So does everything. Everything we've come from and tried to get past. He's not speaking, and I nod, for both of us. Taking that step that could change every fucking thing. "Yeah, dude. That would be fantastic. We'd love to talk."

The guy grins and slips us a business card and we exchange numbers, scribbling mine on the back of a cocktail napkin. He promises to call and then he's gone, slipping into the crowd and swallowed up, carrying the promise of so fucking much in his back pocket.

I look at Scott and laugh when I see the stunned look in his eyes. Sometimes, laughing is the only way to keep from breaking down.

It breaks the shock that's fallen over him and then he's screaming and I'm screaming, and the girls are laughing, shrieking as we pull them into the hug, celebrating everything that could possibly go right. She's got her arms around my neck, the scent of her hair in my nose, legs wrapped around my waist, and my best friend is happier than I've ever seen.

The real shit might be scary as fuck, but it's hella worth it.

"I love you," she whispers, and my grip on her tightens.

Something I learned quick is that watching us perform turns both girls on. Sex with Peyton is always good—fucking fantastic—but when I'm coming off the stage, the girl can't keep her hand off me. It's the same as when we practice at home—they both love it and practice used to get cut short by one of us making out with one of the girls before someone ended up naked.

"When you're rich and famous, you still going to want me?" she murmurs, and even though she's teasing, it sends a fission of unease down my spine.

"Always, Fish. You're it. My always. You forget me, and walk away and I would love you still."

She pulls back, and stares at me, eyes wide and searching. "Do you think I could forget you?"

I shrug. "Doesn't matter. I'll remember for both of us, and I'll make you remember too."

She kisses me then, that deep kiss that I fucking love, the one she controls with her hands in my hair and teeth nipping at my lips before her tongue tangles with mine and everything falls away in a wave of sunshine and sugar and everything that is her.

"Want you," she pants when she pulls back.

It's all I need to hear. I'm moving before she kisses me again, and I hear Scott laughing behind me, but it barely registers as I carry her through the bar to a dark hallway. She squeaks against my throat, her teeth digging in just a little as I bump into a door and then we're spilling into a stockroom that's almost pitch black, and I'm letting her slide down my body, cupping her ass as she falls.

I fucking love her ass in those skin tight jeans she wears when I perform. She's got a corset-looking top on over the jeans, baring a smooth sliver of her belly, and my fingers skim it before I skate lower and cup her, grinding the heel of my hand into her through the jeans.

"Not playing fair," she gasps, and I groan as her hands cup my erection. Stroke and tug in that way she has—not too hard, but rough. Enough to remind me that she wants this just as bad as I do.

She unzips my jeans and drops to her knees, taking me deep in her throat before I can process, and then I can't.

The girl is amazing in bed, but I don't think I'll ever get over the sight of her on her knees, her lips wrapped around my cock. She licks at my shaft, her hand slipping between my legs to cup my balls and I struggle to keep still. My hand is on her head, my fingers twisting in her hair and she relents, the suction of her lips tightening as she slides down, until my dick hits her throat.

"I'm going to come," I mutter.

She pulls back and strokes my dick. "That's the point."

"Not like that." I say pulling her up. "As much as I like fucking your pretty mouth, I want your pussy." Her eyes close and she sways closer. I unsnap her pants and work a hand into her jeans and the door behind us opens.

It's dark. Dark enough that they don't know we're here. But I can see her, all wide eyes and flushed skin.

And I can see them. For a heartbeat, I consider saying something. But she's trembling against me, and I know Scott well enough to know he wouldn't care.

I lift an eyebrow and move my fingers, brushing against her clit, and she jolts against me. I lean into her ear, and whisper, so low, I almost don't hear it, "Stay or go?"

She shudders, and wet warmth is covering my fingers as I slide them into her.

"Stay," she breathes against my ear.

I smile against her skin, shoving my fingers into her, and grinding against her clit. "Be quiet, perfect girl," I whisper.

Then I twist us, so she is against the side wall. In the darkness, we can both see them.

"Watch," I murmur, and she shivers, her eyes on our best friends as Scott drops to his knees, shoves Lindsay's skirt up, and covers her with his lips. Peyton's whole body shudders, her pussy clenching on my fingers as I lazily finger-fuck her, and I grin. Lindsay is biting her hand, trying to stay quiet as he licks her cunt, but it's not working. Tiny noises are leaking out, these gasping little whimpers, and his name, and it's hot as hell.

And Peyton is so fucking wet. I pull my hand out of her pants and she makes a quiet mewl of displeasure, her hips rising and falling restlessly as I work her jeans down to her knees. I glance over at Scott and Peyton. Her head is thrown back, one leg hooked over his shoulder.

I lean into Peyton, and lick her once, feeling her body go tight as she bows off the wall toward me. I grin, and her hands find my hair, pulling me to her. She's on tiptoes as I go to work, my tongue sliding through her, nipping at her clit, searching for the little friction I'm not giving her, and then I do, pinching her clit lightly as I tongue-fuck her and she's coming, her pussy clenching in waves around me.

"Like that, baby?" I hear, and I freeze as Peyton shudders, thrusting against me, her orgasm tripping into another. Lindsay answers Scott in a low murmur, and I hear him groan before he kisses her.

Fuck. Peyton isn't the only one turned on by this shit.

I stand quietly, and lift Peyton just a little.

Lindsay screams as Scott slams into her, her back thudding against the wall, and he groans again, that noise I've heard a million times when we shared women. Peyton is gasping as I grab her ass and fuck her slow and silently, her eyes wide and staring at Scott thrusting into Lindsay.

It's hot as fuck that she's getting off on this, but she is. She's clenching and coming, these continuous orgasms that fall into each other, and she's so wet I can feel it on my balls. I grit my teeth and drop my head into the crook of her neck, biting her shoulder to keep silent.

"Turn me," Linds demands suddenly and he laughs, slowing. He pulls out and she moans, her voice rising to a shriek when he shoves his fingers into her.

"You're demanding," he mutters, and she whimpers, pushing back against him.

He slams into her and she shrieks, a noise he cuts off with a curse and a hand across her mouth, yanking her head back by the hair and hissing, "Quiet, sweetheart. Or I stop."

"Don't you fucking dare," she mutters.

Peyton makes a little huff of air, and I slide a hand between us, toying with her clit as I fuck her. "You like listening to them, sweetheart? Watching Scott fuck her. You love it."

Her eyes find mine, and I see guilt there—mixed with the glassy desire is conflicted guilt, and I lean into her, kissing her hard and fast. "I love everything about you, Fish. Even the dirty girl who plays rough and likes her sex dangerous. You want him to watch me fuck you?"

Her body shakes, answering me for her as she shatters into another orgasm, and on the other side of the room, Lindsay whimpers, a long, drawn out noise as Scott hisses her name. I look over at them—we both look—and I come as Peyton pulls me into her, biting my chest hard as she rides out the climax, and we watch them orgasm.

It's hot and dirty, and for a long moment, the room is silent except for the sound of us breathing. Scott moves first, sliding out of Lindsay, and I swallow my groan as he reaches between her legs, cleaning her up with his hand before he brings his fingers to his lips. She watches as he cleans his fingers and Peyton gasps when Lindsay goes up on tiptoes to kiss him.

Scott's head lifts, and I shift Peyton, shielding her before Scott slaps Lindsay's ass. "Come on, babe."

She grumbles but they put themselves back together and she slips out.

Just before he does, his gaze darts to us, too knowing and serious.

Then the door shuts and closes off the noise of the bar. I slip free of Peyton and she redresses quickly and gives me a curious look. "What was that last thing?"

I shrug. "Scott's a kinky bastard." She arches an eyebrow, and I grin. "Guess I can't really point fingers on that account."

"No," she says dryly. "Not really."

I pull her into me and kiss her. Her hands come up to grip my arms, and when I pull back, it's to lean my forehead against hers. "Are we ok?" I ask softly.

She nods and brushes my lips again. "Always, Jokes."

Chapter 26: After

Being with you is never

Easy.

It's long nights and

Cryptic answers, and Constant challenges.

(Rike's poems to Peyton)

Being back at the house is like living someone else's life. The first few days are awkward as I navigate around Scott and Rike. They're both busy for the first two days after I arrive, building ramps and supervising the crew moving Scott and Lindsay's bedroom downstairs. I drift between them, trying to find where I belong. The problem isn't them. They both are quick to include me in all their conversations, ask me what I want to do and eat and if there's a movie or a song I want to hear—they're so quick and eager, it's almost suffocating.

And when I do snap at them and slap them back into their place, they regard me with wide, hurt eyes. Like I just smacked their puppy instead of their feelings.

That happens four times before I retreat into my loft studio and hide there for most of a day. Rike comes twice to check on me, but it's a cursory thing. He's distracted. And I understand. We both get it. I'm here for Lindsay and the family the four of us created, more than I am for him.

Or. That's what I keep telling myself.

The truth is, I'm here for both. Lindsay is allowing me to come back under a pretense that gives me some dignity instead of me calling and sobbing that I miss him. Because I did. I don't think I realized how much I missed him until I'm back, and he's everywhere and nowhere, a constant fucking presence that keeps me grounded and high.

It's a little disconcerting. And I would never admit this to anyone—except perhaps Lindsay—but I love it.

"Babe?"

I blink as Rike appears at the top of my staircase. I'm sitting in front of an easel, working on a watercolor that hasn't really taken shape for me yet. I've been sketching since I hugged Brody goodbye in Austin. This is the first time since I woke up in the hospital that I've touched paints. His eyes go wide as he takes that in, and I see the struggle to not comment. To treat me like I'm just the girl he's been with forever, and not the mental case we both know I am.

I glance over him—he's wearing faded jeans with a few rips in them, a tight-fitting t-shirt that bares his tattooed arms. His hair is pulled into a messy bun at the back of his neck, exposing his bright blue eyes, sharp cheekbones, and infectious smile.

"Are you going with us?"

I nod, and drop my brush into a vase full of water. Wipe my hands dry on my apron and tug it over my head. "Yeah. Let's go."

Scott is almost vibrating with impatience next to the truck, and he gives me a sick look when we approach. Unexpectedly, for both of us, I give him a quick hug. "Let's go get your girl."

He clings to me for a long minute and when he pulls back, it's with a shaky sigh. He nods and I give him a small smile. Slide into the backseat of the truck while the boys climb in.

"You good, bro?" Rike asks, his voice low.

Scott shrugs. "Let's just go."

Lindsay still isn't committed to coming home. She wants to go to her parents, and call off the engagement. But Jillian told her flat out that coming home wasn't an option. A month. She made Lindsay promise to stay with us for one month, to give her time to get the family home ready for a wheelchair and locate a physical therapist for her. Lindsay bitched and threw a fit, but Jillian was implacable.

When she left the hospital, her daughter screaming behind her, she looked at me and Scott standing outside her door. "You have a month. If anyone can get her back, it's you. Don't waste it." Then she kissed my cheek, hugged Scott and got the hell outta dodge. Leaving us with the furious, sullen girl.

She's sitting in her wheelchair when we arrive. It's actually hers, not a shitty loaner the hospital is sparing for her. It's motorized, and she has a tablet and phone strapped to the side table. It's even bright pink.

"You're late," she says shortly, glaring at Rike. I bite my lip to keep from snapping at her.

Lindsay has always fought with the people she loves, to keep them distracted or to distract herself. Whoever is the safest for her to fight with becomes her target.

I pause in the doorway.

How the hell do I know that? It's not something that was written down in my journals. I shake my head and focus on Lindsay.

She's watching me, and I see hope flare there, and then it's gone. "You came back," she says flatly. I nod and she laughs. "How long are you going to stay this time?"

"Linds," Rike says, his voice sharp.

"It's fine," I say, glancing at him. Calling him down. This isn't about him. I didn't just run from Rike. I ran from all of them, and I ran when she needed me. If I were in that chair, I'd be just as angry.

"I'm here," I say, meeting her angry gaze. "I'm not going anywhere. How about you?"

She glares at me, but she doesn't argue anymore when Scott pick up her bags and we leave the hospital together.

The ride home is tense and silent. Rike talks about a client he's been working on. I've figured out, through a little bit of trial and error, that Rike specializes in large pieces. He'll do anything, but he prefers large tattoos that are heavy on the intricate detail work. He did the mandala on his side that covers an ugly scar that he refuses to talk about.

And I know he sketched the art that Scott has on his back.

The talk of tattoos doesn't do anything to draw Lindsay out of her shell, and we get home in near silence.

The wraparound porch has been added to. A long, wide ramp curves around it, and the patio table has been cleared. Her eyes go wide and she darts a look at Scott before she blinks, going blank. I say, softly, "He's been working hard to make this a place for you."

She shakes her head. "I'm not what he should be working on. He should be on tour by now."

I laugh, and push out of the truck. "He won't go anywhere while you need him."

***

After three days of the four of us in the house, we're beginning to find a rhythm. Rike spends his mornings sketching, and his afternoons with me or Scott. Evenings are for the tattoo shop, before he comes home, tired but happy, and falls into bed to fuck me until we're both exhausted.

Lindsay spends all morning in her bedroom, bitching when Scott drags her to physical therapy. When he retreats to practice with his band, her mood improves and she sits quietly reading or working from her computer while I sketch and write.

And I drift, absorbing everything silently. Every night, Rike watches me with those bright blue eyes, quietly, hopefully, and every day, I have to admit that nothing is changing.

"I think," I say on the third night, while we're lying on the chaise in my studio, catching our breath after sex, "that if I don't remember what we were, it would be ok. That we would be ok. I don't have to remember everything to know that I could be happy with you."

His face softens, and he leans down, brushing a kiss over my lips before he rolls to curl against my back, holding me tight to him. "I want you to remember, sweetheart. I want you to know what we had. But if you don't—you're right. We will be happy. It doesn't change the way I love you."

"Do you think it's easier for us because I wear my scars inside?" I ask.

He sighs and shrugs. Kisses my shoulder. "We can't fight that one, Fish. They'll stand or they won't, and we can only do what we've always done—love them as much as we can, and be there for them."

"What if she leaves? How can I be there for her when I have to be there for Scott?"

"Scott is my best friend. My brother. But Lindsay is yours. And I won't ever stand between that. Neither would he. It might be awkward and uncomfortable, but you'll do what you need to do, to be there for her."

I nod and pull his hand up to brush a kiss over it.

"Does it bother you?" he asks.

I don't need to ask what. "Yes. I wish I knew everything. That I could remember the first time I told you I loved you, or when you said it to me. Our first fight, and when you made love to me, or why we moved here, or—everything. I wish I could remember everything. But that's the past. And the girl I was chose you. The girl I am today is choosing you. So in the end, does it really matter?"

He rolls me and slips into me, easy and effortless. I gasp a little. It never fails to surprise me, how ready he always is. Slow, lazy thrusts have me arching silently against him, and he leans down. I tilt my head for a kiss, but he murmurs into my ear. "In my shitty apartment, after a gig at Barrie's. That's the first time I took you to bed. We had been fighting about the secrets you were keeping, and that night everything changed." He twists, taking me with him as he rolls to his back and I gasp, bracing my hands on his chest as I settle on top of him. "And in the rain. We were camping, and it was raining. And you were dancing in it, like a little girl. We made love in a field, with the rain all around us, and you riding me, and I told you then, because I couldn't stand another minute without you knowing that I loved you. That I will always love you. You're it for me, Fish. The sea and the air I breathe and every fucking thing that matters."

I shatter, gasping his name as the orgasm reaches up and pulls me under, a crashing wave of sensation that begins and ends in him and the steady push and pull of him.

He keeps thrusting, and I lean down, kissing him, grinding against him until he pants my name, his body shaking as he comes.

We lie still for a long moment, wrapped around each other, breathing with each other. "I love you, Fish," he whispers. "Always have. Always will. You remembering that won't change a damn thing for me."

***

Lindsay is in the living room when I come downstairs the next day, and her gaze when it lands on me is miserable. It dims the quiet glow that I've been feeling since last night.

I make two cups of coffee, dumping too much sugar and milk into hers. Grab a Pop-Tart and go back to the living room. I put her coffee in front of her, and curl on the other edge of the couch. Tear open the Pop-Tarts and hand her one.

"Is that something you remembered or something that's muscle memory?" she asks, taking the sugary cardboard.

I shrug. "Let's split the difference and call it a day."

She snorts. I hide my smirk behind my coffee and study her. "So let's talk about you." Her eyes go careful and guarded and I make a noise in the back of my throat. "Don't. Don't do that ice queen bullshit, Linds. I'm here because I'm worried about you. So talk to me."

"You're here because Rike is hot and the sex is phenomenal. Don't delude yourself."

"The sex *is* phenomenal," I say with feeling and she giggles. A real noise that strings hope along me like fireworks.

"Tell me about the wedding," I say.

Tears fill her eyes and she shakes her head. "I can't, Peyton."

"I'm not asking for much, sugar. What colors were you using?"

"Teal and black. My dress was white with a light teal lace overlay and black accents. It was so damn gorgeous." Her voice cracks and for just a second, I think she's going to give in. Let me in. Tell me everything that she's been keeping bottled up and secret. But she takes a sip of her coffee, fighting to get control, and she gives me a watery smile. "It doesn't matter. It's over."

"Why?" I whisper. "Fuck, Lindsay, he *loves* you. The kind of crazy, stop-the-world-from-spinning love that people only dream about. Why on earth are you walking away from that?"

"Because it's the kind of love that stops the world from spinning. And if the world stops spinning, it dies. I don't want him to get this close to having it all, and then throw it away to take care of a cripple who can't be what he needs. I refuse to be the reason he doesn't get his dreams."

I stare at her, stunned by the fierce passion in her voice. By the pure belief that she's right.

There isn't a way to convince her that she isn't. And she isn't walking away because she doesn't love him. Which makes it so much more difficult.

She's walking away because she loves him too much.

Chapter 27: Before

"We should go away," Lindsay says.

I look at her, pulled out of my sketch for just a moment. Peyton is half-asleep, her head on my thigh and my fingers sifting through her hair as I draw.

"Why?"

She looks over her shoulder, at where Scott is banging on guitar strings. He's been in a shitty mood since we came home from Austin two weeks ago. The waiting is killing him.

I understand. It's slowly driving me crazy, and I have the tattoo shop and songwriting to distract me. Scott only has the music. It's always been harder for him.

"Where would we go?" Peyton asks, sleepily.

"My parents' condo."

"You know it's freezing, right?" she asks, a smile in her voice.

"So we wear sweaters and get drunk in the hot tub instead of bikinis and drunk on the beach. Come on. It'll be good to get out of the city for a while, and we're on break. It's perfect."

Peyton peers up at me, her gaze questioning. She's been skittish around Scott for the past few weeks, since that night in the club—and he's noticed, even if he hasn't commented. Shoving us all into a small condo for a few days will either cure her of that or make things worse.

"It sounds fun," I say and she lets out a tiny sigh. "Fine. When do we leave?"

Lindsay shrieks, a happy noise that makes my ears hurt, and Peyton giggles.

"If we leave tomorrow, we can put up a tree and celebrate Christmas!" Linds says, bouncing off the table and darting to her room. "I'm calling Daddy!"

***

It takes less than three hours to get the condo and for Lindsay's father to arrange plane tickets—his present to us, and when we argued, the man was having none of it.

I don't like Peyton's parents, but as parents go, Lindsay did good.

The girls are darting from room to room, stealing clothes and packing and laughing. Scott lands on the couch next to me, his bag on the kitchen table with mine.

We don't need much, and pack fast—a skill I learned in the system that I still carry.

"Think it's a good idea to force Red into this?"

"Why wouldn't it be? She could have said no."

"And you could have said the room was taken."

I go still and Scotty curses. "Dude. You know I don't give a fuck, but it messes with shit. She isn't one of the girls we took home from Barrie's."

"I fucking know that," I snap. "She wanted to stay. So fuck off. She'll be fine."

He looks at me for a minute, skepticism in his gaze, and I growl softly. "I'm not doing anything that will fuck up what I have with her. You ought to know that. She's all that matters."

"What if she doesn't want this? If the next step is signing with this studio and moving to be closer to the indie scene? You know the five year plan."

I do. It's always been the plan—work and build our name in Knoxville before we move to Nashville or Austin.

When we made the plan, it was just us. Two friends with no attachments and big-ass dreams. The girls changed that. I glance at Lindsay as she almost runs past with a sweater and a wide smile. "What about her? Can you let go of her if we leave and she doesn't follow?"

"Lindsay will. She already knows the plan. She's known from the beginning."

I stare at him in shock and he lets out a sharp laugh. "One day, dude, you're going to stop being a distrustful ass, and start letting people in. You might want to do it before Peyton wakes up and realizes how much you don't tell her."

He gets up and follows Lindsay into the bedroom, and I stare at the closed door for a long minute.

Then I stand and walk into our room. Peyton is half in the closet, wrestling a dress off a hanger. She grins at me when she tosses it on the bed, and then stills, staring at me. Her brow furrows. "What's wrong?"

"Would you move with me? To Austin?"

She blinks, her mouth falling open.

She's still so fucking beautiful it hurts. And she's scared. I can see it in her gaze, darting away from mine.

"If this works out, for Scott and me. Would you follow me?"

"Do you want me to?" she asks, her voice shaking.

I move, coming off the bed and catching her around the waist, kissing her hard and fast. "Fuck yes. I love you, Fish. You're everything to me. I don't want you to move with me. I want to marry you. I want you with me forever. I want every vacation to be this mad dash around while you giggle and plan. You writing while I draw. I want you to steal my razor and bitch when I touch your coffee and I want every fucking holiday with you. I want everything, Peyton. I don't even care about the music. I love it, and I love being able to do it with Scott, but if it ever comes down to you or the music, I'm going to pick you. Every fucking time, I'll pick you."

She's leaning against me, her head on my chest, and I can feel her shoulders shaking. When she looks up, her eyes are bright and shiny, but she's smiling, this brilliant fucking smile that makes my insides ache. "Did you just propose?"

I don't even think about it. "Yeah. You saying yes?"

"You fucking idiot," she murmurs, and then she's kissing me, and every fucking thing in my world is right, because she's in my arms.

"Is that a yes?" I ask desperately, and she laughs.

"Of course. It's never been a choice, Rike. I love you—and that means Scott, and everything that come with him. So yes. I'll move to Austin with you. I'll move anywhere. And I'll marry you whenever you're ready."

"This weekend."

She laughs, and she nods before she kisses me.

This. This is the real shit I've been chasing for so long. The family I always wanted and never had. The friends in the other room. This girl, in my arms.

This girl. She will always be everything I've ever wanted.

Chapter 28: After

It's laughter and little lessons and heartbreak.

It is never easy.

But.

Easy is empty.

It's bland and boring. It doesn't make my heart

Sing or dance or hurt.

Easy is empty. And you.

Are everything.

(Rike's poems to Peyton)

The day it happens starts like any other. I've been home for two weeks now, and although we're all working to bring Lindsay out of her shell, to get her to trust us and trust what she and Scott have, it's not working. We can feel her slipping away, and feel him sliding into a deep depression. Rike is fighting to keep him, and Lindsay is vanishing before our eyes.

Rike pops into my studio early this morning, with another cup of coffee and a toe-curling kiss that pulls me instantly from the paints I'm laying out.

I've apologized to my clients, a furious backlog in my inbox that took me a full day to work through. Some I wrote off completely—I couldn't remember enough about the work and the client to put together a solid piece. Others, I offered a discounted price and an apology with a new delivery date. And most were understanding—those who weren't were people I didn't want to work with anyway.

"What are you working on today?" he asks, leaning over my shoulder. He shaved recently, and the beard has since been replaced with an ever-present scruff that I love.

"I'm doing a painting of a wedding photo. They were married in in '62. How long is that?"

"A long fucking time?" he offers, and I laugh.

Look at him over my shoulder. "Do you think we can do that? Be together that long?"

His expression gentles. "Fish. We've been through hell the past three months, yeah? If we can get through this, we can get through anything. Fifty years is a piece of cake."

I nod, and he kisses me again before he steps away. "What about you?" I ask. "What's the plan?"

Rike shrugs. "We're meeting the band about song selection for the next album. Since Scott canceled the tour, they need to get that going to keep the momentum."

"See you tonight?"

He nods, and leans in to kiss me. "See you then."

***

I switch on the radio, and spend the next few hours painting. It's easy to get lost in my art, and it's when I feel closest to the girl I was. Around lunchtime, I go downstairs and make lunch with

Lindsay. She seems alive when I'm the only one home, the depression and walls she puts up when Scott is present melting away until she's laughing and alive.

I make us cold cuts and join her at the table. She's got her computer open and she glances up at me as I sit down. "You're a mess," she says, wrinkling her nose.

"You're one to talk," I tease. "What are you doing?"

She flushes and that piques my interest. "What?" I ask, lowering my sandwich.

"Setting up gigs," she mumbles.

I stare at her and she shifts in her chair. Slaps the laptop shut and glares at me. "Quit staring at me with those accusing eyes. This is for him."

"*He* doesn't want gigs, you idiot. He wants you."

Her lips compress into a tight line. "We aren't doing this," she say sharply.

"Why the hell do you get to tell me that I need to come home and to get my head out of my ass but when I say the same thing, I get shut down and yelled at? Do you want to explain that to me?"

"I want to smack you." She snaps back, "But to do that, I need to walk and we all know the likelihood of that happening."

I let out my breath slowly, and reach for her hand. "Babe. I know why this is scary. But you have a man who loves you. Who wants to be with you. Don't throw it away because you think it's what he needs. Be brave, sweetheart."

She snorts, a disgusted noise. "Like you have been? You've run as far and as fast as you possibly could."

"I came home for you," I say quietly. "And I woke up and realized everything we have. I'm not ashamed of that. You can't make me feel guilty for being happy. Not when we were both happy and can both *be* happy."

She looks so sad. Miserable. "He deserves better."

I stand up. Disgusted suddenly with all of it. With her.

"Who the fuck are you to decide what he deserves? Scotty chose you. He loves you. After all the people who threw him away, all the shit that they both went through—he opened up and trusted *you.* And you're going to decide that he's wrong for making that decision? Fuck you, Lindsay."

I stalk away before she can argue. Before she can fight back at all. Retreat to my studio. The wedding picture is sitting on my table still, quietly taunting me. Emotions are still thrumming through me, all of the fury and frustration. I want to shake her and I want to put our family back together.

I want to know everything I lost.

I reach for a piece of charcoal, and knock over a little curved dish. It clatters as it hits the wood of my studio floor, metal rattling around as it bounces and rolls.

Curious, I pick it up and glance inside.

A small ring clatters there, a brilliant fire opal shining from the center, surrounded by tiny, perfect diamonds. The band is worked with scrolling designs, elegant curves and twists that make my knees weak.

It slips, so, so easily, onto my ring finger, and I stare at it, I start to cry. Tiny tears that slip silently down my cheeks, and fall into my hands. Onto that ring that means everything.

A song is playing. My radio is off, but I can hear it. A song that he sang in a dirty bar, a lifetime ago, to a girl who was scared and running from a family she wanted to forget. I remember sitting in that bar, Lindsay at my side and her telling me to lock him down. The pride and envy in her, the happiness in his best friend's eyes as he found me across the bar. And his voice, crooning a truth I couldn't believe.

I remember falling in love with him that day, and never once looking back. I was his sea, but for me, he was the sun. The light that always guided me home. I couldn't look away from him, because he was everything.

I scramble for my phone. Grab it from where it's sitting on my desk and type the message while the memories crash over me.

Me: *I remember*

Rike: *What??*

The phone rings, and his voice is frantic in my ear, demanding. And I'm sobbing, laughing, the world crashing down around me. "Everything, Jokes. I remember fucking everything."

Epilogue: Now

It's raining, coming down in relentless sheets, and part of me says, *Fuck* this. Stay home. But Scott needs this. We haven't shared the stage in almost a year, since before the accident. After all the shit we've been through, we need it. So we play, and when the crowd is worked up into a frenzy, I take the spotlight, grabbing my guitar and pulling out the song that took us from a tiny bar to this crazy thing that we call real life.

He arches an eyebrow at me and nods to the corner of the room, where a girl with flame red hair and the body of a fucking siren is swaying along to the music. A blonde with glasses and a half-smile sits next to her in a bright pink wheelchair, a small circle of space around them.

The audience knows who they are. They've learned to give our girls room at shows.

"Here's a throwback, to the early days," Scott says and I hit the first chords of her song. The crowd is going crazy, and lighters are in the air. The fans love this shit.

She's smiling, shaking her head just a little. Too amused as I adjust the mic and croon.

Perfect girl,

She sits and listens, And I can't help but see

Everything that she's hiding.

She's beautiful and broken, Tears she tries to hide,

And I can't help but wonder what's on the inside

You're broken and lovely,

Fire and ice,

And holding you is painful,

But the payoff is worth the price,

Because you're everything to me,

Yes, you're everything to me,

Perfect girl.

Everyone said she was wrong, When she danced

to a song only she heard,

And I just want to sing along to the music of her soul,

Because she's beautiful and broken, with the tears she tries to hide.

You're broken and lovely,

Fire and ice,

And holding you is painful,

But the payoff is worth the price,

Because you're everything, to me,

Yes, you're everything to me,

Perfect girl.

And all of us are broken, all of us are flawed,

All of us have battles, and times when we fall.

And I will love you always, with scars and broken heart,

You're beautiful and broken, my perfect girl.

You're broken and lovely,

Fire and ice,

And holding you is painful,

But the payoff is worth the price,

Because you're everything, to me,

Yes, you're everything to me,

Perfect girl.

When we leave the bar, Peyton can't keep her hands off me. Scott and Linds are trailing us. Not everything is smooth there—she's fallen into a distance that bothers me, and even now, almost a year after the accident, she hides behind managing the band. But he's patient and I'm hopeful. One day, her walls will come down, and I'll have my family back, whole and the way it should be.

But for now—I finally have Peyton, and she's here. All of the memories we built, and the love we shared. She said it wouldn't matter. She chose me, even before she remembered loving me. That counted—because we fought hard to find each other, and we did. Twice. It's the kind of thing that doesn't happen. And it did. Sometimes, that kept me awake at night, thankful for things I can't put a name to.

Her head cranes back and she grins at me. "Want to do something crazy, Jokes?"

My eyebrows go up and I smile, slowly. "What'd you have in mind?"

She smirks and prances away from me, twisting to give me a siren smile, the one that's sleepy and sweet. The one I've never been able to resist. The one she gave me in a bar when I fell in love, and on a beach when she promised me forever, and in a hospital when she woke up with no memory and every fucking day since.

"Wanna tattoo your wife?"

Acknowledgments:

As always, I could not have written this book without a host of people.

My mom who babysat and didn't even complain while I wrote through our vacation. My kids who have been amazing with a mom on deadline during summer break, and didn't complain when I listened to the same 20 songs for four months straight.

JC for keeping me laughing and didn't whine when I vanished for a month to write. Deadlines are a beast, babe.

Aj, thank you for listening to all my midnight panic attacks and for pushing me to be better with each story I write. Even the fluffy ones.

All of the amazing bloggers who have read and reviewed and tweeted. Thank you thank you thank you.

A special hug and thank you to Melissa for the gorgeous cover—you blew me away with this one. And to Bri, for making my words look intelligent.

And finally, Jessica. For always being in my corner, with all of book I bring you. This one's for you—and look, no one died! :)

Coming soon:

THE SCION LEGACY

I was just a college student, trying to stay ahead of my student loans. I knew the rules, and I followed them.

I thought I knew how the world worked—humans lived their petty little lives in the safety of the sun. We fucked and fought and—when the sun sank—we scurried behind our walls and lived in fear. That is when the monsters came out to play.

And even in the safety of the sun, we knew who ruled us.

The Houses. And their Scions.

Everyone knows the great Houses and their Scions—they are feared and loved and hated and envied. They are the gods who walk the shadows and rule all of our lives. They are salvation and death.

And somehow, I am one of them.

Join the Legacy...

Fall 2015

About the Author:

Nazarea Andrews is an avid reader and tends to write the stories she wants to read. She loves chocolate and coffee almost as much as she loves books, but not quite as much as she loves her kids. She lives in south Georgia with her husband, daughters, and overgrown dog.

Read More from Nazarea:

The World Without a Future | The Horde Without End

The Future Without Hope | The Ruin of the World

Edge of the Falls | Chasing the Wind

This Love | Beautiful Broken | Sweet Ruin

Girl Lost | Forever Found

Gentle Chains | Violent Freedom (January 2016)

Illicit Desire (writing as Taylor Michaels)